# *Can the Short Stirrup Club help Allie?*

"Well, you'll be back soon," Megan told Allie confidently.

Allie shook her head. "I'm afraid not. The doctor says it'll be months before I can use my hands again for much of anything. I'm no good to the farm this way." She looked at her hands in disgust. "I can't even scratch my own nose, let alone a horse's."

"Well, we're going to help you, Allie," Keith said. "Right?"

"Right," Max said.

"Don't you worry, Allie," Chloe said. "Everybody helped me when my arm was broken, remember?"

"This is a sight worse than a broken arm," Allie said bitterly.

"Never mind," Megan said firmly. "We have a plan."

The kids had agreed to keep the Pony Express fund-raiser ride a surprise, so they didn't tell Allie what the plan was. Before they left, Megan stuck her head around the door to wave at Allie one more time. But Allie's face was turned away. Megan saw a tear run down her cheek and splash upon one of her bandaged hands.

"We'll finish the ride," Megan said to herself. But for the first time since the group had planned the Pony Express ride, a finger of doubt began to poke at her heart. None of them had ever ridden fifteen miles cross-country. Could the Short Stirrup Club really do it?

**Books in the SHORT STIRRUP CLUB™ series** (by Allison Estes)

Available from MINSTREL BOOKS

# Pony Express

## Allison Estes

A MINSTREL® BOOK

Published by POCKET BOOKS

New York   London   Toronto   Sydney   Tokyo   Singapore

A MINSTREL PAPERBACK *Original*

 A Minstrel Book Published by
POCKET BOOKS, a division of Simon & Schuster Inc.
1230 Avenue of the Americas, New York, NY 10020

Copyright © 1997 by Allison Estes

ISBN: 0-671-00435-2

First Minstrel Books printing July 1997

10  9  8  7  6  5  4  3  2  1

SHORT STIRRUP CLUB is a trademark of Simon & Schuster Inc.

A MINSTREL BOOK and colophon are registered trademarks of Simon & Schuster Inc.

Front cover photo by Pat Hill Studio

Printed in the U.S.A.

*To Julianne Caputo, the best groom ever. And with special appreciation to grooms everywhere, whose hard work and diligent care should not go unrecognized.*

"Short Stirrup" is a division in horse shows, open to riders age twelve and under. Additional requirements may vary from show to show.

# Pony Express

# 1

*IT'S SATURDAY!* WAS THE FIRST THOUGHT THAT POPPED into Megan Morrison's head when she opened her eyes. Her bedroom was warm with lemony sunlight, though outside, she knew, the November air was crisp. *It's a perfect morning for riding!* was her next thought, as she hurried to brush her teeth and make up the bed.

Megan threw on a pair of jeans, a turtleneck, a sweater. She raked a brush through the tangled waves of her brown hair and gathered it into a hasty ponytail. Then she grabbed a pair of socks and galloped down the stairs, her bare feet thumping on the wooden steps. Saturday! On Saturdays Megan could spend the whole day at Thistle Ridge Farm with her brother, their friends, and her pony, Pixie.

"Morning, Meg," her dad, James Morrison, said as she went to the refrigerator.

"Mmm," Megan replied, searching for the orange juice. Megan's thoughts raced through her head in the morning, but it wasn't until after breakfast that she became her usual talkative self.

"It's over here," Max Morrison said, pointing to the orange juice carton on the table. Max was Megan's twin brother, but sometimes people could hardly believe that the two were twins. Megan had James Morrison's stocky build and mischievous brown eyes. Max was tall and slim like their mother, with the same light brown hair and blue-gray eyes.

Megan sat down and poured herself a glass of juice. Sipping it, she watched her father making scrambled eggs. He'd been away for a month, painting a portrait of a famous actress. Megan was glad he was home again.

"Mom?" Megan said to her brother. She meant, "Is Mom here?"

Max understood. "She's sleeping," he told his sister. "She had to do an emergency surgery last night."

Megan nodded and drained her juice glass. The twins' mother, Dr. Rose Morrison, was an orthopedic surgeon. The Morrisons had moved to Hickoryville, Tennessee, back in the spring. Dr. Morrison had been hired to run the orthopedics unit at the big new medical center in nearby Memphis.

At first it had been difficult for Megan and Max

2

to leave their home in Westfield, Connecticut, and move to a whole new town in a whole new part of the country. For eleven years, almost her whole life, Megan had lived in the same house, gone to the same school, and known the same kids. Her pony, Pixie, and Max's horse, Popsicle, had adjusted to their new surroundings just fine. But it had taken Megan and Max a little longer to get used to a different barn and a new house. Megan remembered her first few strange, lonely days at Thistle Ridge. Mostly she had spent them wishing she could just turn around and go back to Connecticut, to her old home and friends. But finally she had met Chloe Goodman, a twelve-year-old girl who rode at Thistle Ridge, and now she and Chloe were best friends. Megan looked around her, at the comfortable kitchen, at her brother reading the cereal box across from her, at her father stirring eggs over the stove, and thought, *This is home now.*

Feeling satisfied, she took a bite of the eggs her father had set down in front of her. By the time she had eaten them and a piece of toast, she was ready to go. "Come on, guys," she said to her father and brother. "Let's get a move on! I want to get to the barn."

Max and his father exchanged looks and laughed. "Megan's finally awake," Mr. Morrison remarked.

"Cover your ears, everyone!" Max teased.

"Hmph!" Megan said, pulling on her socks. She plunked herself down on the floor by the kitchen door, shoved her feet into her worn, brown paddock boots, and began to lace them. "Just because you guys can't get yourselves going in the morning is no reason to pick on me!" She stood up, grabbed her jacket off the hook nearby, and opened the kitchen door. "I'll be in the Bronco," she announced. "My pony awaits me."

"Wait a second." James Morrison stopped her. "Since you're the first one out, you might as well warm it up for the rest of us." He held out the keys to the Bronco.

"No, I want to!" Max said. He jumped to his feet and made a grab for the keys.

"No way," Megan said, swiping the keys before her brother could reach them. "You snooze, you lose!" She stuck out her tongue at her brother and closed the kitchen door with a bang.

Outside the frosty air burned her nostrils and the tips of her ears, and her breath came out in clouds. By noon, Megan knew, the sun would be warm enough that she wouldn't need her jacket, but at that moment she was glad of it. The grass, the rooftops, and the Bronco sparkled with frost.

Megan got into the Bronco and closed the door, then started it up and turned on the heater. While she waited for her father and brother, she thought of her pony.

Pixie was a pretty, dark dapple-gray mare. She stood about thirteen hands, two inches high at the withers, which made her a medium pony. She was

**4**

spirited and a little spooky, but Megan didn't mind; Pixie was a wonderful jumper, and Megan loved to jump. She loved how Pixie's ears would prick forward and her strides quicken as she approached a fence. She loved the silent, soaring moment in the air as the pony tucked her feet up to her belly, and the neat landing after they had cleared the jump. Then the sound of Pixie's hoofbeats would start again as they headed toward the next fence.

Megan could hardly wait to get to the barn. She rubbed a clear spot in the foggy window and peered through it impatiently, looking for Max and her father. At last they came. Megan slid over so that her father could take the driver's seat, and they were on their way. The stables were only a couple of miles down the road. Soon Megan caught sight of the white wooden fences that framed the pastures and paddocks at the front of the farm. In another moment they were turning up the tree-lined gravel driveway that led to the main barn. Megan leaned forward eagerly, hoping to glimpse the foals that were usually turned out in the paddock closest to the barn. But the paddock was empty.

"That's strange," Megan said, disappointed. "I wonder why Allie hasn't turned out the babies yet." The clock on the dashboard told her it was seven-forty. Usually Allie Tatum, the head groom at Thistle Ridge, would have finished feeding the horses by seven o'clock. By this time she would have the foals turned out, and any other horses that needed it. If she peeked into the office, Megan knew, Allie would be seated at the big old oak desk, drinking a mug of coffee and making a list of school horses to have ready for the first riding lessons.

"Maybe she's just extra busy this morning, since Sharon and Jake are out of town," Max suggested.

Sharon Wyndham and her husband, Jake, owned Thistle Ridge Farm. The farm was big—nearly two hundred acres of hilly woods and pastures bounded by cedar post-and-rail fences. A creek crossed one side of the farm, a large lake was near the back, and in between were scattered ponds for thirsty horses and cows to drink from. Megan and her brother loved trail riding all over the farm with their best friends, Chloe and Keith.

There were also many buildings and riding arenas on the farm. Besides the huge green-shuttered main barn, there was a summer barn, a hay barn, and a tractor shed. There were big and small indoor and outdoor arenas, a longeing ring, a dressage ring, and a hunter ring like a grassy field, set with natural jumps. All those rings were busy nearly every day with people taking lessons, trainers working with horses, or boarders schooling their own horses. There were horse shows at Thistle Ridge every couple of months.

Such a large, busy farm needed capable hands to run it. Pretty, blond-haired Sharon, a three-time Olympic rider, trained horses and riders for careers in show jumping and dressage. Megan felt lucky that Sharon trained her and Max.

Jake Wyndham raised cows and handled the practical side of running the farm. With his border collie, Merlin, he could usually be found somewhere on the property, slinging a hammer, digging postholes, or overseeing the men cutting hay.

Besides Jake and Sharon, there were several grooms who helped out around the place and took care of the horses. But when Megan thought about who really made Thistle Ridge Farm run, the person who came to her mind was Allie Tatum.

Allie had been the first friendly person Megan and Max had met at Thistle Ridge Farm. In the months that followed, Allie had continued to be unfailingly friendly and caring. Whenever the kids were going to ride their horses and ponies, Allie would find a moment to check the girths and the fit of the bridles. Other grooms were hired to muck out stalls, but as often as not, Allie could be seen hefting pitchforks full of dirty bedding into a wheelbarrow. Allie could get a horse groomed and tacked faster than Megan could believe, and pull manes, braid, and trim a horse's ears and whiskers faster than anybody Megan had ever seen.

Allie handled even the most difficult, spirited horses with a quiet strength and assurance that Megan hoped one day to possess. Whenever there was a problem of any kind—a horse that wouldn't load up onto a trailer, or a horse that wouldn't unload, a horse that looked colicky or lame or too hot or too cold—Allie was always there, helping out in her frank, fearless way.

Megan knew her own pony very well. But Allie knew every inch of every single horse in the barn, all their likes and dislikes, their bumps and scars. She knew the special spots where they liked to be scratched or rubbed and exactly how hard or soft to rub them. Allie called all the horses her "kids," and horses responded to her as with no one else. When Allie spoke, fidgety horses stood still and good horses behaved better. Nervous horses lowered their heads and snorted with relief, and surly horses put their ears forward and listened politely.

Allie was the first to arrive at the farm in the morning and the last to leave in the evening. She never seemed to need a rest, and if she caught any kid just hanging around with nothing to do, she'd give that kid a job. More than once Megan had been wandering around the barn looking at the horses and suddenly found herself cleaning tack or sweeping the aisle. But, Megan had to admit, she had learned an awful lot from the chores Allie had given her.

Allie had taught the kids how to take apart and put together a bridle. She had shown them different kinds of bits and explained how they worked. Best of all, Allie let the kids catch the foals and lead them back to their stalls in the evening, as long as she was there to supervise. Megan's favorite foal was Eclipse, a little bay filly with a white crescent moon on her forehead. Eclipse was still recovering from the terrible cuts she had received when she'd gotten tangled in a barbed wire fence. Megan shuddered. She didn't like to remember how she'd found the little filly caught there, or worse, how Eclipse had gotten out in the first place. She pushed the thought aside and instead remembered how grateful she had been when Allie had let her help care for Eclipse. Allie had taught Megan to clean the filly's cuts and change the bandages. Little by little, the cuts had begun to heal, and Eclipse had come to trust Megan although she still shied when strangers approached her.

Most of the kids who knew Sharon Wyndham or were lucky enough to ride with her thought Sharon was the best trainer in the world. Megan thought so, too. And, she knew, Jake Wyndham was just as good at helping to run the farm. But Megan always thought of Allie Tatum as the heart of Thistle Ridge Farm. Allie was so good at everything that had to do with horses that Megan sometimes wondered if Allie could be part horse!

"Maybe Allie decided to leave the foals in today," Max suggested from the backseat. "It's pretty chilly out this morning. Or maybe she turned them out in another paddock."

"Maybe so," Megan agreed. She checked her jacket pocket. Had she remembered to bring treats?

Then she found them: half a bag of baby carrots for Eclipse, and a roll of peppermints for Pixie.

Their dad dropped Megan and Max at the top of the driveway. "I'll see you later," he told them.

"Take your time, Dad," Megan offered cheerily. Once she got to the barn, Megan never wanted to leave.

Max looked at Megan. "Let's go," he said, and the two kids went into the barn.

Megan held herself to a fast walk. She couldn't wait to see her pony, but she knew better than to run in the barn. She hadn't gone more than a few feet when she realized that something was different in the barn. For one thing, the lights were off. Then she noticed that the horses were all acting disturbed. The barn should have been filled with the peaceful sounds of horses finishing up their morning grain, and the rustling of their hay as they munched it in sweet mouthfuls. Instead, Megan heard horses snorting and pawing impatiently, and kicking the walls of their stalls. Some of them nickered urgently when they saw her and Max. Megan's steps slowed as she looked around her, trying to figure out why the horses were acting so peculiar. She stopped, listening uncertainly.

"Max," Megan said, putting a hand on her brother's arm to stop him.

Max stopped, a curious expression on his face. "What is it?"

"I'm not sure, but . . ." Megan shook her head

slowly, still listening to the agitated horses. She made a puzzled gesture with one hand. "Listen," she told her brother. A strange, uneasy feeling had begun to creep into her through the cold floor. It started at her feet, then ran up her spine, turning into a chilly shiver of dread when it reached the back of her neck.

The bad feeling was all around her then, but not quite visible, like a strange smell, or an unfamiliar sound in the night. She stood rooted to the spot, anxiously searching the barn with her eyes while she waited to discover what it was. Was someone in the barn, hidden in the shadows, upsetting the horses? Or was it some *thing?* And why was the barn so dark?

"Something's very wrong," she said to Max.

# 2

MAX FOUND THE LIGHT SWITCH AND SNAPPED IT ON. Cheerful brightness filled the barn. The horses began to whinny then, and the stomps and kicks grew louder. Max walked over to the nearest stall and peered into it. He moved to check the next stall. "Meg," he said, after checking one more stall, "I don't think anyone fed the horses this morning."

That was it! That was why the horses were all disturbed. Megan knew that the horses were used to a regular routine. They expected to be fed at a certain time. They knew it was way past feeding time, and they were trying to tell someone. But why hadn't the horses been fed?

One of the barn cats, a half-grown gray tabby, twined itself around her ankles in a ceaseless figure eight. Megan stooped and picked up the little cat.

It purred too loudly, kneading her with its claws. The barn had the strange, empty feeling of a place normally full of people who suddenly aren't there. Where was everybody? Usually Sharon would be there, but she and Jake had gone on a horse-buying trip. They wouldn't be back until Monday. Megan glanced at the barn clock. It was nearly eight o'clock. The early grooms came in at eight on weekends, to start getting the school horses ready for the first lessons. They would be arriving any minute, she guessed. But Allie should have already been at the barn. Where could she be?

"Max, let's check and see if Allie's truck is here," Megan suggested. She put the kitten down. It mewed plaintively at her. Megan realized the cats hadn't been fed, either. She found the dry cat food and poured it into the dish. Two other half-grown kittens from the same litter came scampering toward the sound of the food, along with Fancy, their mother. Megan paused to scratch Fancy's brindle head before she followed her brother through the stables.

The two kids went around to the side parking lot where the instructors and barn staff usually parked their cars. Except for Jake's blue Ford pickup, it was empty.

"Where do you suppose she is?" Max said.

"I don't know, but I'm not getting a good feeling about this," Megan said. "Have you ever known Allie to be late?"

13

"Never." Max shook his head emphatically. "She just never would be. Something must be wrong."

"I hope it's nothing bad," Megan said, twisting her clasped hands nervously. "Maybe her truck broke down on the way to the barn," she suggested hopefully. "Or, she could have had a flat tire."

"Maybe," Max agreed. "Or maybe she just overslept."

"I bet she'll be here any minute," Megan said.

"I hope so," Max said.

Megan felt better. She had an idea. "Max, let's start feeding the horses for Allie!" she said. "You know Allie—she's probably freaking out that she's late. Let's get the horses fed, so she can relax when she gets here."

"Okay," Max said. "Anyway, they're going to kick the barn down if someone doesn't feed them soon," he added, as another grumpy, hungry horse stomped in his stall.

"Come on, then," Megan said, pulling her brother in the direction of the feed room.

In the center of the feed room was the feed cart: a big green plastic bin on wheels, with a handle to push it with. Megan lifted the cover and saw that the bin was full of the feed most of the horses ate, a mixture of oats, pellets, and molasses-sweet feed. Allie always filled the cart before she left at night, so it would be all ready when she came in early in the morning. Megan tugged on the handle of the feed cart. She was going to back out the door

**14**

with it, but she barely budged it an inch, it was so heavy.

"Max, help me," she said, tugging uselessly at the heavy cart.

Max took hold of the handle beside his sister, and with both of them pulling as hard as they could, they managed to pull it out the door of the feed room. "Man, this thing is heavy!" Max said, grunting as he struggled to maneuver it so that it was facing down the aisle. "I can't believe Allie could move this thing around all by herself."

"Allie's strong," Megan said.

"No kidding," Max said. "Well, where do we start?" He flipped open the top of the feed cart and picked up the scoop inside.

Posted on each stall was a card that told what to feed each horse. In the first stall was a school horse called Hot Shot. "This says, 'two-two mix,'" Megan read. "What does that mean?"

"It means he gets two quarts of mixed feed in the morning and two in the evening," Max said. "Don't you know that?"

"I do now," Megan said. "How do you measure a quart?" she asked, eyeing Hot Shot, who was pawing impatiently.

"This scoop equals one quart," Max said.

"How do you know?"

"How do you think?" Max replied. "Allie taught me." He plunged the scoop into the feed mixture and measured two scoops into a bucket. Then he

**15**

slid open Hot Shot's door and dumped the feed into the horse's grain bucket. Hot Shot nearly dove into the bucket, attacking his breakfast with his ears laid back. The horse in the next stall pressed his nose against the bars separating the top halves of the stalls. Hot Shot kicked out, his metal shoe slamming the wall, warning the horse in the next stall to stay away. Max backed out of the stall fast, closing the door after him.

Megan laughed. "What's the matter, little brother? You're not scared, are you?"

"No, I am not scared," Max said defensively. "I just have better sense than to hang around a horse who's that hungry!" Max went back to the feed cart. "Who's next?" he asked.

"Quasar," Megan said. Quasar was one of Sharon's Olympic horses. Sharon had won a gold medal riding Quasar in the Three-Day event at the Olympic Games in Atlanta that summer. "It says he gets three quarts, plus corn oil. How much corn oil, I wonder." Megan studied the feed card.

"Allie usually just splashes some on top of his feed," Max said. "Here." Max handed her the bucket. "I'll measure, and you feed. It'll go faster that way."

Megan took the feed bucket. A plastic jug of corn oil hung from Quasar's stall. She poured some on top of the feed. "That was two 'glugs.' You think that's enough?"

Max laughed. "That sounds about right," he said.

16

Megan poured the feed into Quasar's bucket. His manners were completely different from Hot Shot's. Quasar began to nibble his feed earnestly. She watched him for a moment, thinking how each horse really had his own distinct personality. Then she gave Quasar's shiny chestnut neck a pat and closed the door.

"Next," Max said.

"Prince Charming. One and one. Bran mash," Megan read. "Uh-oh, he still gets bran mash, because of his surgery. What do we do?" Prince Charming belonged to Amanda Sloane, a twelve-year-old girl who rode at Thistle Ridge Farm. The horse had survived a terrible colic episode a few weeks before. He was recovering just fine, but still needed a bran mash every day.

Another horse whinnied impatiently. "Should we skip him, and just keep feeding the others?" Max asked.

Prince Charming looked hopefully at them. His ears were so far forward they nearly touched at the tips. His whiskery lips quivered hungrily as he watched the two children. He nickered softly. "Oh-hoho, ple-he-he-he-hease," he seemed to say. "Plehehease feeed me!"

Megan had to laugh. "Look at him, Max," she said. "How can we skip him?"

Max hesitated. "I'm afraid to give him his feed without the bran mash."

**17**

"Maybe we can just give him a handful," Megan said. "So he won't feel left out."

While they were trying to decide, Jenny Grantham, one of the grooms, came into the barn. Jenny, a senior in high school, was a working student at Thistle Ridge. She groomed and schooled horses in return for her lessons from Sharon. When she saw Max and Megan with the feed cart, she stopped. "What are you guys doing?" she asked.

Megan was glad that someone older and more knowledgeable had arrived. "We got to the barn early, and the horses hadn't been fed yet, so we were starting to feed them," she explained.

"How do you know they haven't been fed?" Jenny asked, looking into a stall as she spoke.

"I checked," Max told her. "The buckets are all empty."

"You're right," Jenny said, checking one more stall to be sure. "Where's Allie?" she asked, coming back to stand beside the twins.

"We don't know," Megan said. "When we came in, nobody was around. The lights weren't even turned on."

"Hmm," Jenny said. "That's strange. It's not like Allie to be late. Did you try to call her?"

"We didn't think of that," Max said. "We figured maybe she had a flat tire or something. The horses were all acting crazy so we figured we'd better get them fed."

"Is it okay?" Megan asked. Suddenly she was

worried. Maybe they should have waited. "The horses were so hungry. . . . We've been reading the feed cards carefully," she added.

"Oh, it's fine," Jenny reassured her. "As long as you know what you're doing. Why don't you keep on feeding? I'm going to try to call Allie, then I'll come and help you," she said.

"Oh, Jenny," Max said. "It says Prince Charming is supposed to get a bran mash, but we don't know how to make one."

"Oh. I can fix that." Jenny turned and went into the second aisle of the barn, where the wash stall was. In a few minutes she came back, carrying two big buckets full of wet, steamy brown stuff. "I always leave it in the wash stall, ready for Allie to mix in the morning," she explained. "One of these is for Prince Charming, and the other is for Willow," she said, setting down the buckets. "There's one more bucket sitting in the wash stall. That's beet pulp for Cinnamon. I'll be right back to help you." Jenny went into the barn office to call Allie.

Max dumped a scoop of feed into Prince Charming's bran mash, and Megan poured it into his bucket. The big white horse began gobbling his breakfast. Megan watched him fondly for a moment. "You're so handsome," she murmured. "I wish I could have another horse. I would choose you," she told him lovingly.

"Megan, hurry up, will you?" Max interrupted. "We have a lot of horses to feed."

**19**

Megan said good-bye to Prince and hurried to feed the next horse. She was in the stall when she heard the screen door of the office bang shut. She stepped out and saw Jenny coming toward them, looking worried.

"Did you reach Allie?" Max asked.

"No," Jenny said. "For some reason I kept getting a recording that said her phone was temporarily out of service. I hope nothing's wrong." She glanced at her wristwatch. "It's just not like Allie to be so late."

Megan helped Max push the feed cart further down the aisle. It was getting a little lighter since they had fed about half the horses. Jenny got another bucket and handed it to Max. "Here," she said. "Let me measure, and you two feed. We can do it faster that way."

The three of them moved quickly down the aisle, Jenny measuring out the feed for each horse and Max and Megan dumping it into the buckets. Megan began to enjoy herself. She was surprised at how different the horses' diets were. Horses got more or less feed depending on their size, their age, how much work they did, and what kind of work. Some horses got different things added to their feed, like corn oil, or special mineral additives, or vitamins. Some got pellets instead of the mix. Bo Peep, the pretty black Exmoor pony, got only a handful of sweet feed.

Soon they had finished feeding all the horses in

the main aisle. It was time to start feeding the horses in the second aisle, but the feed cart was almost empty.

"I tell you what," Jenny said. "I'm going to start watering in this aisle. Can you two go on and finish feeding in the second aisle?"

"Sure we can," Max said.

Megan nodded vigorously. "Of course. But the feed cart's almost empty. How do we fill it up?"

"Come on, I'll show you," Jenny said, heading for the feed room. Max and Megan followed, dragging the feed cart behind them.

In the feed room was a square metal spout that came down from the ceiling. It had a little sliding door across the bottom. The children watched as Jenny positioned the feed cart underneath the spout. She slid the door open, and the feed mixture began pouring down into the cart.

"The feed storage bin is above us," Jenny explained, keeping a close eye on the feed spilling into the cart. It was filling up fast, making a golden brown pile. "When the storage bin runs low, a big truck comes and fills it up again, through a special door in the top. That way we don't have to deal with loading and unloading all those heavy bags of grain."

"Cool!" Megan said, looking up at the ceiling. "I never knew they stored the feed like that."

"In our old barn we had those bags of feed," Max said.

21

"How much feed is up there?" Megan asked.

"It holds a couple of tons," Jenny replied.

The cart was almost full. With both hands, Jenny pushed the door halfway closed, slowing the flow. When the cart was full, she closed it completely. Megan noticed that the door seemed sticky. Jenny had to wiggle it a little to get it to slide closed.

Jenny helped them push the cart into the second aisle. "Okay, I'm going to water," she said. "Don't forget Cinnamon's beet pulp."

"We won't," Megan assured her. The horses in the second aisle whinnied hungrily when they heard the first ring of the scoop slicing through the feed, and the feed singing as it poured into the bucket. Megan recognized her own pony's voice among them. "Hey, Pixie girl," she called. Pixie let out a tiny, squeaky whinny that shook her whole body when she heard Megan's voice.

Megan laughed. She would have known that whinny anywhere. Just like people, each horse had his or her own voice.

When they had finished feeding the horses, Max got the hose and started filling the empty water buckets. Megan took the empty cart back to the feed room and parked it under the chute. She started to leave it there, but then remembered that she had found it full. "I guess I ought to fill it up," she said to herself. She pulled the sliding door open and the feed poured out in a golden brown column. It began to form a hill in the bottom of the cart.

Megan leaned over the edge and watched, fascinated. The hill of feed would build up to a small mountain, then the top would slide down the sides, flattening itself out. Then another peak would quickly form.

When the cart was nearly full, Megan realized she'd better shut off the flow. She took hold of the little door that closed off the chute at the bottom and pushed it. It didn't move. She pushed harder, wiggling it as she'd seen Jenny do. It moved about two inches, then seemed to stick. Growing nervous, Megan wiggled some more, then pushed really hard on it. The feed cart was completely full. It would overflow if she didn't close the chute.

But the little door wouldn't slide any farther. Megan realized that the weight of all the feed pressing down on it was making it hard to close. She thought maybe if she pulled it all the way open again, then slid it really fast, it would close. She pulled it back. For some reason it slid easily that way, and before she could stop it, the little door had slipped completely off its track!

Megan stood for a second in complete surprise. She held the useless door in her hand while the feed continued to stream out of the chute. Then she frantically tried to put the door back on its track. The feed rushed over her trembling hands and tumbled over the sides of the cart onto the floor. Megan struggled with the little door. Every time she thought she had it back on the track, the

23

feed would push it off again. Panicked, Megan glanced down. The floor around her was covered with spilled grain a couple of inches deep already. It seemed to be coming out of the chute faster and faster.

She looked at the ceiling. Above the chute was all that grain, tons of it. And it would keep pouring down, piles and piles of it, unless she could get the chute closed off. She gave up trying to put the door on its track. Instead she tried to stop the flow by pushing the door against the bottom of the chute. But she wasn't strong enough to hold it there. Next she dropped the door and covered the opening with her own hands. The grain pounded down relentlessly, beating them away.

"Max?" Megan called fearfully.

A haze of golden dust hung in the air, choking her. She coughed. The grain kept piling up. What if it blocked the door and she couldn't get out? What if she were trapped? She would be buried under all that feed! "Jenny, help!" she called frantically. There was no answer. She took a deep breath. *"Maaax!"* she shrieked, still trying desperately to cover the chute with her hands as the feed rained down around her.

# 3

THE FEED HAD PILED UP KNEE HIGH AROUND THE BOT-
tom of the cart, and the pile kept spreading and
growing. At last Megan gave up trying to stop the
stream of grain. *"Max! Jenny!"* she yelled, as she
waded toward the door. The heavy grain was hard
to walk through. She reached the door, twisted the
knob, and pulled. "Oh, no!" she wailed, as she realized what had happened. The door opened inward,
and it was blocked by the feed on the floor. Megan's worst fear had come true. She was trapped!

Megan couldn't remember ever being so scared,
not even the time she thought she saw a ghost in
the old barn in the back pasture. She dropped to
her knees and began raking the feed away from the
bottom of the door in double handfuls. Then she
tried the door again. This time she got it open an

25

inch. She sat down, wrapped her fingers around the edge of the door, and tugged as hard as she could. It opened another couple of inches, but not enough for her to squeeze through. She glanced behind her and was frightened all over again by the huge pile of grain. It loomed behind her, pushing toward her, growing and spreading like something alive. Megan began to scream.

Frantically she pulled at the door, but it was no use. It wouldn't open any farther. A draft of fresh air from outside teased her. The feed was getting deeper. It pushed at her back. Megan was crying now. *"Max, Jenny, Maaaaax!"* she called, coughing every few seconds.

"Megan? What are you doing in there?"

Megan sobbed with relief at the sound of Jenny's voice. At last someone had heard her. "The feed chute is open, and I can't close it!" she yelled. "Get me out of here, please!" she begged.

"Max, come here, quick!" Jenny said. She peered in at Megan through the slim opening. "Don't worry, Megan, we'll get you out," she said calmly.

But Megan saw the alarm in Jenny's face. She kept her fingers in the crack, and held on with all her might, struggling to keep the door from closing.

"When I count to three, shove," Jenny ordered Max. "One, two, three!"

Megan heard them both grunt as they threw

26

themselves against the door. It moved an inch toward her.

"Again!" Jenny shouted. "One, two, three!" They hit the door. "Megan, can you pull some of the feed away from the bottom of the door?" Jenny asked.

"I'm afraid to let go of the door," Megan said. "If I do, it will start to close again."

"We'll keep it open," Jenny promised her. She shoved her knee in the crack and leaned against it. "Go on, hurry," she urged Megan. "If you can move some of that feed away, I think we can open it."

Megan hesitated for a second. She looked at Jenny's knee holding the door open, then let go and began raking the feed away from the door with both hands. When she had cleared as much as she could, she told Jenny.

"Okay, on three, we'll push and you pull, hard," Jenny said. "Ready? One, two, *three!*"

Megan pulled as hard as she could. At the same time, Jenny and Max slammed into the door. To Megan's relief, it opened a few more inches. She quickly turned sideways and squeezed through the opening, tumbling into Jenny and Max.

"Are you okay?" they both asked her.

Megan nodded, then coughed, breathing the fresh air gratefully.

"What'll we do about the feed?" Max asked Jenny.

"There's not much we can do," Jenny said, peering in through the opening. "Except hope the over-head storage bin wasn't full!"

A few moments later, the last of the feed slid through the chute. Megan peeked into the room and saw a huge pile of grain. It had buried the feed cart and spread into the corners of the room, filling the space waist high.

"Wow," Max said. "What a mess."

"You're not kidding," Megan said gloomily. She had just about stopped crying, but looking at the huge pile of spilled feed, she felt her eyes well up all over again. It was all her fault. She felt terrible.

"Hey, the important thing is you're not hurt," Jenny said kindly. "It's not your fault the chute wouldn't close. It could have been worse."

Megan managed a small smile through her tears. She was relieved that Jenny wasn't going to make things any worse by yelling at her for being so stupid. "What'll we do about all that feed?" she asked.

"I don't know," Jenny said. "I guess Jake will have to figure something out when he gets back. I'm going to start tacking up the school horses. Try and stay out of trouble for a few minutes, will you?" Jenny winked good-naturedly at Megan and went to get her grooming kit.

"Hey, y'all!" Chloe Goodman said. She had just walked into the stables. Her cheeks were very rosy from the cold, and the ends of her white-blond hair stuck out from under a brightly colored crocheted hat.

"Hi, Chloe," Megan said, glad to see her friend.

Chloe saw how serious everybody looked. "What's the matter?" she asked.

When they told her what had happened, Chloe's green eyes grew wide with alarm. "Oh my gosh!" she exclaimed. "Megan, are you okay?"

"I'm fine," Megan said. "I just feel bad about this big mess I made."

"What mess?" It was Keith Hill, Max's best friend, who had come in after Chloe. Keith's longish hair was as shining dark as his eyes. He had the tan skin and features of his Native American and Mexican parents.

"Wow," Keith said when he heard about Megan's adventure in the feed room. Then he grinned. "Megan, you're the only person I know who can stir up that much excitement before nine o'clock in the morning. How do you do it?" he teased.

"I don't know." Megan shrugged. In a Count Dracula voice she said, "Wherever I go, danger stalks me. But restless spirits, wild horses, and even avalanches of falling grain cannot stop me." Her voice rose dramatically. "For I am—Megan Morrison: Danger Pro!" She made a grand gesture with one arm, as if she were sweeping back an imaginary cape.

Chloe, Max, and Keith all laughed. Megan joined in, relieved that the disaster in the feed room was over. But then she caught sight of someone, a bedraggled figure standing just inside the barn door, and her laughter died on her lips.

"Allie . . . ?" Megan said in astonishment.

The other kids stopped laughing, too. They all stared at the lone figure. It was Allie Tatum—Megan could tell by her stance and the shape of her shoulders, the same way she could recognize a horse from a distance by its outline. But if it hadn't been for that, Megan wasn't sure she would have known the young woman at all.

Allie was wearing gray sweats, but it was hard to tell, because her face and clothes were covered with some kind of black stuff. It looked like soot, Megan thought. Allie's wavy brown hair tumbled wildly around her shoulders. She wasn't wearing a coat, in spite of the cold, and for some reason she had only one sneaker on. The other foot was bare and red with cold under the black smudges.

"Allie, what happened to you?" Megan blurted out. "You look terrible!"

Allie's arms hung limply by her sides. She took a staggering step toward the children. Megan saw that her blue-green eyes were brimming with tears.

"I'm late," Allie said, in a voice that sounded raw and raspy. "I'm so sorry," she croaked in a hoarse whisper. Suddenly she sank to her knees. She made no effort to catch herself, but sat down limply on the cold concrete, as if that were the only thing to do. "My hands," she whispered, staring at her palms.

"Oh!" Megan said, shocked. Allie's hands were red and blistered.

"Oh, Allie, your hands!" Chloe said, running to kneel by Allie.

"Get Jenny," Max said tensely to Keith.

Keith stood still, as if he hadn't heard. He was staring at Allie as if she were some kind of alien. Max thumped him in the chest.

"Unh," Keith grunted. He blinked.

"Go get Jenny," Max hissed. He gave Keith a little push in the direction Jenny had gone. Keith stumbled away, looking back over his shoulder at Allie, who still sat on the cold barn floor.

"What happened to her?" Max asked softly.

"Her hands are burned," Megan said. "Look."

"She shouldn't be here on the cold floor," Chloe said. "Help me get her into the office."

Max and Megan ran to Allie's side. The three kids managed to help her up and into the office. They sat her down on the old leather couch. Then Jenny burst into the room, with Keith right behind her.

Jenny froze when she saw Allie's condition. But only for a second. She grabbed the phone and called 911. When she had given the operator all the information, she ran to Allie's side.

"Allie, what happened? How did you burn your hands?" Jenny asked her.

"I don't know," Allie said hoarsely. She didn't look at any of them, but seemed to be staring at something far away. "My house," she whispered in her broken voice, and tears began oozing out of her red-rimmed eyes.

The paramedics came quickly. Fifteen minutes later, Allie was on her way to the hospital. Jenny went with her. The kids sadly watched the ambulance disappear down the drive, then spent the whole day wondering what had happened. They groomed their horses and exercised them, but nobody's heart was in it. Even Megan, who was happiest when she was on her pony, couldn't enjoy the ride because she was too busy worrying about Allie.

It wasn't until later, when Jenny came back from the hospital, that the kids learned the whole story. Allie lived in an old woodframe house she had inherited from a great-aunt. Sometime very early in the morning, before sunup, Allie's cat, Bandit, woke her up.

Bandit was crying loudly and clawing at the covers. Allie sat up in alarm. Her room was filled with thick, choking smoke. She knew the house was on fire. She grabbed Bandit and crawled down the stairs toward the living room.

Allie was almost to the front door when a burst of flame sprang up before it, blocking the door. The terrible smoke filled the room. It seared her throat until she could hardly breathe, and stung her eyes until she couldn't keep them open anymore. Confused, she tried to feel her way out of the living room, but couldn't get her bearings. Bandit scratched and struggled under her arm until she had to let him go.

But the cat did not run away. He stayed near her, meowing loudly as he led her out of the fiery living room. On her hands and knees she followed Bandit's cries until she found her way into the kitchen, which wasn't yet on fire. Groping by the kitchen door, she found one shoe. Then she searched for her truck keys but couldn't find them.

The flames had found their way to the kitchen by then. Allie gave up looking for the keys and was about to leave the house when she remembered Bandit. She thought she heard him somewhere nearby, meowing pitifully. She couldn't leave him, so she groped her way toward the sound, calling for him. But it must have been the fire singing as it burned its way through her house. She didn't find the brave little cat, and the meowing cries had stopped.

Allie crawled back to the kitchen, but by then the flames had spread. They formed a roaring wall before her, licking at the kitchen door. Allie knew she had to get out then, or it would be too late. She plunged through the flames and managed to unlock the door and get out, to safety. But her hands were badly burned.

Allie had watched helplessly while the fire fighters tried to save her house. But the flames gobbled the old, dry wood. By dawn, only a black, smoking skeleton of the house remained. The fire fighters said that probably the electrical wiring was old and had started the fire.

In the chilly morning light, Allie had turned away from the remains of her home. And not knowing what else to do, she set out on foot for Thistle Ridge Farm.

"Poor Allie," Megan whispered, when she heard the whole story.

"I can't believe she walked all that way with only one shoe on and no coat," Keith said.

"What happened to Bandit?" Chloe asked. "Did he get out of the house by himself?"

"Allie never found him," Jenny said.

"He saved her life," Chloe said soberly. "If he hadn't woken her up and led her into the kitchen, she might have been killed in the fire."

"That's true," Jenny said.

"Poor Bandit," Chloe said. She held her chin high, her eyes glistening.

"How's Allie doing?" Max asked.

"The doctor says her hands are in bad shape," Jenny said. "She's not going to be able to do much of anything with them for quite a while."

"What about farrier school?" Megan asked.

Allie had been saving up her money to go to farrier school. She was going to learn to shoe horses, like her Uncle John, who had shod the horses at Thistle Ridge for nearly twenty years. She had finally saved up enough money to pay the tuition, and had just started taking courses.

Jenny shook her head sadly. "She's not going to be able to finish this semester at farrier school. It looks like she's going to have to go live with her parents while her hands heal."

"Where do they live?" Max asked.

"Somewhere in Mississippi, I think," Jenny told the kids.

"You mean, Allie's going to leave Thistle Ridge Farm?" Megan was incredulous. She simply couldn't imagine Thistle Ridge without Allie.

"It looks that way," Jenny said.

"What'll we do without Allie?" Keith asked sadly.

"Yeah, she practically runs this whole farm," Max said. "Except for Jake and Sharon," he added.

"This place will fall apart without Allie!" Megan protested. "She can't leave."

"Maybe it won't fall apart," Chloe said softly, "but it sure won't be the same without her."

A tear dripped out of Megan's eye and rolled down her cheek. How could such a terrible thing happen to someone like Allie? She looked around at Jenny, and at the other three kids, and saw that nobody's eyes were dry.

# 4

"I wish there was something we could do to help Allie," Keith said.

"I know!" Max said eagerly. "We could do her chores for her."

"It's a nice idea," Jenny said. "But most of the work Allie does around here isn't stuff that kids can do—handling stallions and moving hay bales around is grown-up work."

"I could handle Cuckabur!" Megan protested. Cuckabur was Sharon's stallion, who stood at stud when he wasn't in training for the Olympics.

"Oh, sure you could," Max said skeptically.

Jenny shook her head. "Stallions are wacky. It would be too dangerous for a kid."

"But you forget," Megan said. "I am Megan Morrison, Danger Pro!"

Chloe giggled. Then she said, "I guess we couldn't handle Cuckabur, but we could do the rest of Allie's chores."

Jenny frowned. "I doubt your parents are going to drive you to the barn at five-thirty every morning to feed the horses."

Chloe's face fell. "You're right."

Megan sighed. "I just feel so bad for Allie. I wish there was *something* we could do."

"Unless you've got a few thousand dollars to pay her tuition to farrier school for the next semester, and a few more thousand for her to live on until her hands heal, I'm afraid about all you can do is feel bad," Jenny said. "But if you want to help out right now, you can go up into the hayloft and drop about a half dozen bales for me. It's time to feed."

"Okay," the kids said. Megan glanced guiltily at the feed room. It had take Jules, another groom, most of the morning to shovel all the spilled feed into a pile in one corner.

A wooden ladder led to the hayloft, where bales of hay were neatly stacked in golden rectangles. Megan loved it up in the loft. It was peaceful, and the sweet smell of the hay reminded her of summer—of the green pastures growing under the warm blue sky.

The four kids took turns throwing hay bales off the stack and pushing them across the floor toward the door of the hayloft. When they had six bales ready, Keith opened the little door. Cool air streamed in, along with a pinkish-gold shaft of afternoon sunlight.

Megan peered down at the area below, just outside the far end of the main aisle, where they were going to drop the bales. When she was sure that no people were there, she announced, "The coast is clear."

"Heads up," Max yelled. He slid the first bale to the edge of the doorway, then tipped it over. It fell to the ground with a satisfying *whump*.

"Me next!" Keith said. With a running start, he slid his hay bale across the wooden floor and out the door, where it fell on top of Max's bale and bounced aside.

"My turn," Megan said. She pushed her bale to the edge and shoved it over. "Geronimo!" she yelled gleefully, as she watched it tumble down. She could never figure out why dropping hay was so much fun, but it was.

Chloe slowly slid her bale off the edge. It fell gracefully, doing one flip before landing on top of the growing pile of bales.

There were two bales left to drop. "Come on, Max," Keith said. "Let's go down and start haying the horses. Megan and Chloe can drop the other two." The boys started down the ladder.

Chloe pushed a hay bale toward Megan, who shoved it out the door. The last bale had only one piece of baling twine around it. The bale had begun to spread out like a fan on the side where the twine had popped off. Chloe pushed it at Megan. "Care-ful," she cautioned. "This one's coming apart."

"Got it." Megan carefully pushed the bound edge of the bale into the doorway and tipped it over the edge. Just then a girl walked out of the barn, right underneath where they were dropping the hay! Megan tried frantically to hold on to the slippery bale, but it was too late.

"Amanda, watch out!" Megan shouted, to warn the girl below.

Amanda Sloane looked up, saw the hay bale fall-ing, and simply screamed, rooted to the spot.

Megan closed her eyes, wincing when Amanda's scream was abruptly cut off. There was silence. The heavy hay bale had fallen right on top of Amanda. Megan cringed, sure she would see Amanda lying on the ground unconscious when she looked over the edge.

She slowly opened her eyes and peered down, expecting the worst. To Megan's relief, she saw Amanda sitting up in the same spot where she had been standing a moment before. Luckily the loose bale had broken apart when it hit Amanda. It had knocked her down, but she wasn't hurt, only stunned—and completely covered with hay.

Megan began to laugh. Amanda looked up at her and Chloe, where they perched in the doorway of the hayloft. Scowling, she spit out a mouthful of hay.

"Amanda, are you all right?" Megan said through

her giggles. She hadn't meant to drop the bale on top of her, but she was enjoying seeing snooty Amanda Sloane in her fancy riding clothes, sitting on her butt, covered with hay.

Amanda sneezed. "Well, if I am hurt, my daddy will probably sue you," she grumbled.

"Sorry!" Megan called down to her. "Man, that was a close one," Megan whispered to Chloe.

"You're not kidding," Chloe said.

"Come on, let's go help Max and Keith with the haying," Megan said, starting down the ladder.

Released from the strands of baling twine that bound them, each bale of hay came apart into eight or ten sections, called flakes. The four children worked quickly, giving each horse two or three flakes of hay. Megan started to open the door of a stall to put the hay in. Then she remembered that she had seen Allie throw the hay to each horse in a perfect arc over the tops of the stalls. It saved the trouble of opening and closing each door.

Megan decided to try it. She gathered two flakes of hay and flung them toward the top of the stall wall. But the hay didn't go over the wall and fall into the stall as she had planned. Instead, it went straight up and then fell straight down, right on top of her.

The hay flakes broke over her head, scattering all around her. Megan was left standing empty-handed, with bits of hay clinging to her hair and clothes.

"Nice shot, Meg," Max said, laughing. Keith was holding his stomach, doubled over with laughter. Even Chloe couldn't help giggling at her.

Megan had to laugh herself. Then she noticed that Amanda Sloane had seen it, too, and was enjoying it more than anybody. Pieces of hay and dust still clung to Amanda's perfect blond braids. "Guess I deserved that, huh, Amanda?" Megan said good-naturedly.

"You two look like a couple of scarecrows!" Keith chortled.

"Thanks," Megan said, brushing herself off. She picked up the scattered hay and opened the stall door. "I guess I'm not as strong as Allie," she said, tossing the hay into the stall.

Everybody grew quiet when she mentioned Allie. Megan wondered again if Thistle Ridge Farm would ever be the same. Suddenly she had an idea. She slid the stall door closed and turned around to face the other kids. "You guys, we're calling an emergency meeting of the Short Stirrup Club."

The Short Stirrup Club was made up of Megan, Max, Chloe, Keith, and Amanda. They called themselves that because they all showed in the Short Stirrup division in horse shows. The kids listened curiously as Megan went on.

"We've got to figure out a plan to keep Allie at Thistle Ridge Farm. You know how much she loves it here, and how much we all count on her. This place would never be the same if she left. There's

**41**

got to be some way we can help her," she said with determination. "Short Stirrup Club to the rescue!"

When the Short Stirrup Club had finished haying the horses, they met in the barn office. It seemed lonely and empty without Jake or Sharon or Allie around. The only sound in the usually busy office was the old wall clock, ticking away. It reminded Megan that they needed to come up with a plan to help Allie, and fast.

Keith and Chloe plunked themselves down on the creaky, cracked leather sofa. Max quickly took the old wooden office chair behind the desk. Megan was sure he did that to escape from Amanda, who was always trying to sit next to him, talk to him, or invite him over for dinner. Amanda watched Max sit down in the chair and, with a disappointed pout, went over and arranged herself on the couch next to Chloe.

Megan stood before the group. "Okay," she began. "Point one. Allie's got no place to live. Point two—"

"Why doesn't she?" Amanda interrupted.

"Why doesn't she what?" Megan said.

"Why doesn't she have a place to live?"

"Because her house burned down," Keith said. "Didn't you hear about it?"

"Well, I heard she was in a fire," Amanda said. "But I didn't know it was her house. I thought she lived here."

"Point two," Megan went on, ignoring Amanda. "She saved up her money to go to farrier school, and now she can't finish the semester. She'll have to go back and start that all over again when her hands get better. But she'll have to pay the tuition again, too, and she can't save up the money if she can't work."

"Why can't she work?" Amanda wanted to know.

"Because her hands got burned in the fire and it's going to take a long time for them to get better," Megan explained. "Which brings us to point three: Allie needs help."

"Big time," Max agreed.

"What can we do?" Keith asked.

"Well, we've got to come up with a plan to raise money for her," Megan said.

"I know!" Chloe said. "We could make up a whole bunch of those big pickle jars with labels on them that show Allie's picture and tell what happened. Then we can leave them all over town, in stores and restaurants. I just saw one at the Beacon Diner where my mom works. They're trying to raise money for a boy who needs a kidney transplant."

Megan frowned. "It's a good idea, but do you ever see anything but pennies and nickels and quarters in those jars?" she asked.

Max shook his head. "People just throw in their loose change. It would take a long time to make all the jars and distribute them, and even longer to collect enough money to really help."

"How much money do you think we need to raise?" Keith asked.

"Well," Megan said, "Jenny said the tuition at the farrier school is about five thousand dollars. And Allie needs money to live on for a while, for groceries and rent and stuff. I figure that we should try to raise about ten thousand dollars," Megan announced.

The kids all looked at each other, except for Amanda, who was busy studying her fingernails. They were painted with bright blue polish.

"Where are we going to come up with ten thousand dollars?" Max asked skeptically.

"Well, I've got a hundred and seventy-seven dollars saved up from baby-sitting. I'll put that in," Chloe offered. "But ten thousand? That's an awful lot of money. I'd have to baby-sit until I became a grandmother to raise that much money."

"Max and I have some money in a savings account," Megan remembered. "Keith, how much have you got? Maybe if we put it all together, we'll have enough to help."

Max shook his head. "Meg, we're supposed to be saving that money for college. Mom and Dad are never going to let us take it out."

"Mine, too," Keith said. "I don't think my parents would let me touch it, even for Allie. Maybe we could have another gymkhana show," Keith suggested. "We raised enough money to go to the Olympics last summer. And we had some left to donate to the handicapped riding program," he reminded them.

"We raised about seven hundred dollars," Megan said. "That's nowhere near enough."

"If only we knew someone we could get to donate some money," Max said thoughtfully.

"Yeah, like some rich guy who could afford to just hand over ten thousand dollars . . ." Keith said, his eyes drifting sideways toward Amanda, who sat primly admiring her blue nails.

Megan, Chloe, and Max all stared at Amanda, too. Megan knew they were all thinking the same thing. Amanda's father, Gerald Sloane, was one of the richest men in Hickoryville. He was running for mayor, and it was almost election day. Would Mr. Sloane donate ten thousand dollars to help Allie Tatum?

Megan wasn't known for keeping quiet. She plunged right in and asked, "Amanda, what about your dad? Would he donate money for Allie?"

Amanda glanced around at the hopeful faces of the other kids. Megan could never tell what Amanda was thinking behind her pale blue eyes. Then she spoke. "Well, I'll ask him, but he's awfully busy right now. You know he's running for mayor."

"Great! That's just great, Amanda," Megan said enthusiastically. "Isn't that great, you guys? Amanda's dad can donate the money for Allie."

"Wait a minute," Max objected. "That's not necessarily true. Amanda said she'd *ask* her father. That doesn't mean he's going to do it."

Chloe agreed. "I don't think we can count on Mr. Sloane. We need to come up with another plan."

"I guess you're right," Megan said gloomily. "But what?" She sat down on a corner of the big oak desk and sighed.

# 5

THE FIVE CHILDREN FELL SILENT, EACH TRYING TO THINK of some way to raise the money for Allie. Even Amanda stopped admiring her nails and looked thoughtfully up at the ceiling. While they were considering, the office door opened, and Jenny and Jules, the grooms, came in.

Jules wore a pair of faded red coveralls to protect her clothes. Her long, wavy black hair was caught in a loose ponytail, which fell over one shoulder in a shiny curtain when she bent to tighten the lace of one of her work boots. Then she straightened up and stood, hands on her hips, her brown eyes sparkling as she demanded, "What's the matter with you guys? You don't look like five kids with horses and ponies of your own that you can ride whenever you want. What're all the glum faces?"

47

"Yeah, what are you guys doing in here?" Jenny asked them. "Shouldn't you be out there kissing your ponies' noses, and blowing on their feet?" She winked at Chloe, who had been known to clean every last speck of dirt from her pony's feet by blowing on them.

Chloe grinned self-consciously. "I already did his feet," she admitted.

"We're trying to think of a way to raise some money to help Allie," Max explained. "But so far we haven't got any really great ideas."

"We thought about collecting money in those big jars you leave in stores and restaurants," Chloe said.

"And Amanda's going to ask her father if he would contribute," Megan said.

Jenny shook her head. "You can't just go around asking people for money. Even if they would do-nate, Allie probably wouldn't accept charity. Can you actually imagine someone like Allie letting you put her picture on a pickle jar?"

"I guess not," Chloe said.

"What you need to do is have some kind of a fund-raising event that people would enjoy. Then they'll contribute their money willingly, and it won't feel so much like charity to Allie," Jenny suggested.

"Oh yeah, like the AIDS walk or the March of Dimes," Jules said, "where you participate in a fun thing, like the big walk, and you get people to sponsor you for however many dollars per mile."

"Jules, that's a great idea!" Megan said. "We could do our own walkathon for Allie."

"Now you're talking," Jules said. "You plan this walk, then you go out and get people to pledge their money. I bet five smart kids like you can get a lot of sponsors. You'll raise the money in no time," Jules said confidently.

"I bet you're right," Megan said. "Oh, it's perfect! Let's get some paper and start writing down plans right away." She took paper and a pen from the desk, then paused. "What should we call this project?" she asked.

Chloe spoke up. "What do you think of this?" she asked. "Do y'all know about the Pony Express?"

Chloe, who read every book she could find on the subject of horses, had been reading about the Pony Express. She explained how, in the late 1800s, the American West was still wild. California was settled and its cities were growing and booming, but all the land between there and the Mississippi River was dangerous, unsettled country. The people in California had to wait weeks and even months to send and receive mail and supplies, which were delivered by slow boats that sailed around the Isthmus of Panama, or by freight wagons pulled by teams of oxen.

"Suppose we wanted to send a letter from here in Hickoryville to someone in California. How long

did it take to get mail from the East to the West?"
Megan asked.

"By boat or by freight wagon, about twenty-five
days. Sometimes longer," Chloe told her.

"Wow, that is slow!" Keith remarked.

"That's what the people in California thought,"
Chloe agreed. "They were tired of feeling so cut off
from their relatives and friends back east. So this
senator from California got people to sign a peti-
tion saying they wanted an overland mail service
that would bring them mail faster. The government
set up a stagecoach route called the Butterfield
Overland Mail service. But that service ended up
being just as slow as the boats. That's when a
freight company operator named William Russell
thought up the idea of the Pony Express.

"Listen to this, y'all," Chloe went on excitedly,
pulling a folded sheet of notebook paper from her
pocket. "I wrote this down so I could remember all
the facts. This is so interesting. . . ." She unfolded
the paper and began to read. "The first Pony Express riders took off from St. Joseph, Missouri,
heading west and from Sacramento, California,
heading east on April third, eighteen sixty. They
didn't take the slower southern route that the Butterfield Overland and the freight wagons used. Instead, they followed a central route that was seven
hundred sixty miles shorter. It took them across
the great plains, where they were chased by Indians, through terrible desert regions and over

treacherous mountain passes. But they carried the mail one thousand, nine hundred sixty-six miles in just ten days."

"Wow!" Megan said.

"Amazing!" Max exclaimed.

"How many riders and horses were there?" Keith wanted to know.

Chloe said, "In all, there were eighty Pony Express riders. Most of them were young men under eighteen years old and weighing less than a hundred twenty pounds. There were about five hundred horses, and they were the best horses that could be found for the job," Chloe went on. "For the flat prairie country, they chose thoroughbreds, and for the dangerous mountain and desert crossings, they used sturdy mustangs. The horses were mostly under fifteen hands high, and many were mares."

"Yay, mares!" Keith put out a hand, and Megan slapped it, because they both owned mares.

"The horses were fed the best grain and hay, to keep them in top condition," Chloe continued. "The riders soon found out how important that was. They couldn't carry much more than a knife and a small gun to protect themselves from Indian attacks, so they relied on their horses' speed. Most of the time the grass-fed Indian ponies couldn't catch the speedy, grain-fed Pony Express horses."

"How far did each rider go?" Max asked.

"There were one hundred ninety stations set up

all along the route. The swing stations, where a rider changed horses, were about ten or fifteen miles apart. That was about as far as a horse could gallop without a rest. At the station, the rider had two minutes to throw the mailbag, called the *mochila*, onto a fresh horse and ride on, but most of them made the switch in about thirty seconds. The rider would change horses at each station until he reached his home station, where a fresh rider would start out. Home stations were usually over a hundred miles apart," Chloe said.

"Oh my gosh!" Megan said. "I can't believe they rode that far."

"Oh, some of them rode even farther." Chloe told them some of the stories of the greatest Pony Express riders and the fastest runs. There was "Pony Bob" Haslam, who completed a 120-mile run with his jaw broken by an Indian arrow and his arm shattered by bullets. There was Howard Egan, who found the trail through a narrow canyon blocked by Indians and simply galloped right through them. Warren Upson spent more than a day struggling through snowdrifts higher than a man's head to get through a mountain pass to the next station. And there was William Cody, "Buffalo Bill," who was barely fifteen when he made one of the longest runs ever recorded, 384 miles in less than twenty-four hours.

"I love to gallop," Megan mused, "but I don't think I could do it for that long."

"How long did the Pony Express last?" Keith asked.

"Just a little over eighteen months," Chloe said. "But in that time, it carried thirty-seven thousand, seven hundred fifty-three letters on three hundred eight runs over a distance equal to twenty-four times around the world! Only one *mochila* was ever lost. Only one rider was killed by Indians, but his horse escaped with the *mochila* and completed the run."

"Awesome!" Max said.

"In October eighteen sixty-one, the transcontinental telegraph line was completed. Then people could send telegrams across the United States. That pretty much ended the need for the Pony Express," Chloe finished.

"It's kind of sad, isn't it?" Jenny said. "In those times, people considered the Pony Express riders just as brave and important as the space shuttle astronauts are today. Then all of a sudden, nobody needed them anymore."

"Just think," Jules said. She calculated in her head for a moment. "If you drove a car that distance straight through, averaging sixty miles an hour, it would take you about two days and a night. That's if you didn't have to stop for gas or food. Those guys did it on horses, riding at all hours of the day and night, in all kinds of weather, through all kinds of danger. And they did it in only ten days!"

"The fastest trip ever was only seven days and

seventeen hours!" Chloe remembered. "That was in March of eighteen sixty-one, when the Pony carried the news of the election of President Lincoln."

"That's awesome!" Keith said.

"I never realized the Pony Express was so important," Max said.

"It's really cool," Megan agreed. "But we need to get back to planning our walkathon." She picked up her notepad and pen again.

"Hey, I have an idea," Keith said. "Instead of a walkathon, how about a ride-athon?" he suggested. "Riding our horses would be more fun and interesting than if we just walked."

"We could cover a lot more miles if we rode," Max mused. "And the more miles we ride, the more money we raise."

Suddenly Megan had an idea. "Chloe," she said, "are you thinking what I'm thinking?"

"Why do you think I told y'all all this stuff about the Pony Express?" Chloe said.

"We can have our own Pony Express!" Megan nearly shouted. She was so excited she jumped off the desk.

"That's a great idea!" Keith stood up. "We can plan out a route and switch horses and riders at stations, just the way the real Pony riders did!"

"Jenny and I will help you guys, won't we, Jen?" Jules said.

"Absolutely," Jenny agreed. "We'll be at every station to help take care of your horses when you ride in."

Megan's mind was already racing with plans to put their idea into action. "Okay, okay," she said, pacing back and forth in the little office. "First we need to plan our route. Then we need to figure out how to get the horses to the stations."

"Well, the way I see it, you need to have Jake or somebody load up the horses in the big trailer," Jules said. "Then he can drive ahead and be waiting at each station to pick up one horse and let off the next."

"How many miles do you think we can cover?" Keith asked. "I mean, we can't do a hundred miles like the real Pony Express riders."

"I bet we could each do ten or twelve miles, though," Megan said. "That was the distance between the stations, wasn't it, Chloe?"

Chloe nodded. "We'll have to do this thing in one whole day, because you know they're never going to let us ride around at night," she said.

"We could start at the town square, right in front of the courthouse," Keith suggested.

"I think it would be better to end there," Max said.

"Why don't we start *and* end there?" Megan suggested. "I bet we could circle the whole town in a day. What do you guys think?" She turned to Jenny and Jules.

"Part of the old Natchez Trace runs along the

outskirts of Hickoryville," Jules said. "The real trail, not the highway. I hiked it once. A horse could travel it safely."

"What about the rest of the route?" Jenny asked. "Do you think they can make it around the town without a trail to follow?"

Jules nodded. "I bet they can. I know the area pretty well, because I've hiked it so much. The only real problem I can see is if they have trouble crossing fenced-in pastures. But if we plan it carefully enough, it shouldn't be a big deal to figure out where they can pass through gates."

"As long as you close them afterward," Jenny said, looking pointedly at all the kids.

"Enough talk!" Megan said. "Come on, guys, put your hands in," she said, holding out her hand.

Max, Keith, and Chloe came forward immediately and added their hands to the pile. Only Amanda hesitated.

"Come on, Amanda," Megan said. "You're with us, aren't you?"

Amanda spoke up. "I don't want to ride."

"But why? Don't you want to help Allie?" Chloe asked her.

Amanda nodded. "But I'm scared to ride Prince Charming through the woods all by myself. What if I get lost?"

"We'll have a map to follow," Megan said. "It won't be that hard. Just think of it as a long jump course," she added.

"I forget jump courses," Amanda pointed out.

"That's true," Megan agreed. "But you can do this," she argued.

Amanda shook her head. "I'm too afraid. You know I'm not such a great rider."

The other kids exchanged looks. It was true; Amanda wasn't a very strong rider. She had done well in horse shows because she had ridden great horses, not because she was especially talented. But it was surprising to actually hear her admit it. Megan had always assumed that Amanda thought she was one of the best riders at the stables. She looked at her with new respect.

"But Amanda," Keith said, "you wanted to be in the Short Stirrup Club. That means you have to join in when we decide to do something like help Allie out, or whatever."

"I will help," Amanda said. "I just don't want to ride."

"But, Amanda, that's what we're doing!" Megan objected. "How are you going to help if you don't ride?"

"Wait a second," Jenny said soothingly. "There must be some way Amanda can help out even if she doesn't want to ride."

"Here's another angle for you," Jules said. "You kids get as many pledges as you can for your ride. You figure out how much money that will add up to: say it's five thousand dollars. Then you go to some guy like Amanda's father and you say, 'Look,

we raised this much money, will you match it?'
That way, he doesn't feel like you're just trying to
milk him for his big bucks. And I bet he'd be will-
ing to put up a lot of money if you promise to tell
people to vote for him for mayor."

Jenny nodded. "That's the kind of stuff politi-
cians really go for. Especially around election time.
I bet he'll be glad to match whatever you raise, if
you just make sure to publicize it so he looks good.
Amanda, do you think you could help us by speak-
ing to your father about this?"

"I'll talk to my daddy and see if I can get him to
put in a whole lot of money," Amanda promised.
"But I'm not going to ride," she said firmly.

"Okay, fair enough," Megan said.

Amanda laid her hand on top of the pile, and the
five kids cheered, "Short Stirrup Club!" The revival
of the Pony Express had begun.

# 6

SHARON AND JAKE WYNDHAM CAME BACK FROM THEIR trip on Monday. They were saddened and shocked when they heard what had happened to Allie. When Megan told them about their fund-raising idea, they agreed to help in any way they could.

Jake provided an aerial map of the town of Hickoryville and the land surrounding it. With Jenny and Jules's help, the kids marked out a route that they divided into four sections, beginning and ending at the town square.

"It's long," Jenny cautioned them. "You're each going to cover more like twenty miles, instead of ten or fifteen."

"The first rider will have to start early, as soon as the sun comes up," Jules told them. "You won't be going at a gallop the whole way, like the real

Pony riders, but you can't take your time, either, or the last rider won't finish by dark. But the way I figure it, if you don't get into any trouble on the way, you should just make it."

"This is going to be so cool!" Megan said excitedly. She felt a little thrill rush through her. She could already imagine darting through the woods on swift, supple Pixie, bending in and out among the tree branches.

The kids started training for the ride, to build up their own stamina, as well as their horses'. They took long trail rides all over Thistle Ridge Farm, trotting up and down the rolling hills.

Keith was worried that it would be too much for Penny, his mare, because she was pregnant. But Dr. Pepper, the veterinarian, assured him that she would be just fine, as long as he built up her strength gradually.

Megan made Amanda come with them on the training rides. She told Amanda that even though she wasn't planning to ride, she should be ready as a backup, just in case. "By the way, Amanda," Megan asked her, as they trotted up a long hill. "What did your dad say about the money?"

Amanda shifted uncomfortably in the saddle. "I didn't ask him yet," she admitted.

"But why not?" Max demanded. "You promised to."

"Yeah, we're really counting on you to get your dad to help out," Keith added.

"Amanda, why haven't you asked him yet?" Chloe said in surprise. "We've only got two more weeks until the ride."

Amanda hung her head. "I started to the other day, but then I just couldn't," she said. "He's such a grouch, now that it's getting close to election day."

"We'll all ask him, then," Megan said with determination. "Together."

That was how, the next afternoon after school, Megan found herself, along with her brother, Keith, and Chloe, pedaling up the steep hill that led to the Sloanes' house. They left their bikes in the front yard and marched up to the front door of Amanda Sloane's huge home.

"I've always wondered what the inside of this house looks like," Chloe whispered, gazing in awe at the three-story house that towered above her.

"It looks more like a castle than a house," Keith said. His eyes followed a trail of English ivy up the stone walls to the steep green roof far above.

"I bet that her bedroom is huge," Chloe said reverently.

"Which window do you think is hers?" Megan asked, searching for a girlish curtain that could mark Amanda's room.

"Which windows, you mean?" Chloe said. "I bet her room takes up about a whole half a floor."

"Who cares?" Max said impatiently. He reached past Megan and punched the doorbell. The first phrase of "Dixie" rang out in an ominous minor key.

Keith and Max looked at each other and snickered. From somewhere in the unknown reaches of the house came the deep barking of a large dog. It came closer and closer, along with the sound of someone's footsteps.

"Max, be quiet!" a voice said, from behind the door.

Megan remembered that the Sloanes' dog was named Max. She grinned impishly at her brother, who scowled and looked away. Megan knew Max was embarrassed that people would think Amanda had named her dog after him.

Then the big door opened with a creak. There stood Amanda, holding a huge, snarling German shepherd by the collar. The dog lunged and barked again. Startled, Megan took a step back.

"Oh, don't mind Max," Amanda said airily. "He's just playing. Come inside." She stood aside, and the four children stepped uneasily into the foyer. Then Amanda closed the door, letting go of the dog's collar. The German shepherd ran to Chloe and, standing up on his hind legs, put his huge paws on her shoulders.

Megan thought she was about to see her best friend devoured by a German shepherd. The big dog growled low in his throat as he looked Chloe in the eye. Chloe did not move. Then, to Megan's surprise, the dog began licking Chloe's face with great affection.

Chloe laughed and patted the big dog. Then she took his paws off her shoulders and scolded him. "Now Max, you know you're not supposed to climb up on people like that." She scratched him behind his ears. Max flopped down upon the cool marble floor and rolled over, showing his creamy belly. Chloe scratched it for him, and all the kids laughed as one of the dog's hind legs twitched helplessly in enjoyment.

Relieved that Max wasn't going to attack, Megan and the other kids followed Amanda through the house and into the living room, where Amanda's father was.

Gerald Sloane lay back in a big green recliner, shoes off, tie loosened, snoring mightily. His top lip wiggled each time he let out his breath. Megan had to cover her mouth to stifle a giggle. She looked around and saw that the other kids, including Amanda, were doing the same.

Max the German shepherd put a huge paw on Mr. Sloane's shoulder and licked the sleeping man's face. Mr. Sloane batted at the dog with one hand. "Go on, Max," he said, an annoyed expression crossing his face. But Max kept licking him. Mr. Sloane opened his eyes.

"What are y'all doin', standin' there starin' at me like that?" he demanded. "Pamela! There's a whole bunch of children in here, and I'm tryin' to sleep!"

He twisted his head around, looking off in another direction. "Pamela!" he bellowed.

Pamela Sloane was Amanda's mother. Megan couldn't stand her. Nobody could. Megan was relieved when Amanda told her father, "She's not here, Daddy. She's playin' golf."

Mr. Sloane looked at the children in dismay, as if he had suddenly been assigned some task that he had no wish to complete. "Well, what do you want me to do about it?" he said impatiently.

Megan sensed that if there was a good time to ask Mr. Sloane for something, this was it. She plunged right in. "Um, Mr. Sloane? We came to talk to you about something important. Something that has to do with your running for mayor," she added hastily, to get his interest.

"Is that right?" he asked. "Well, what is it?"

"I guess by now you must have heard about Allie Tatum," Megan went on.

"Her house burned down, Daddy," Amanda said. "Isn't that just terrible? And she's all alone in the hospital, with no place to go."

"Her hands were burned in the fire, so she had to drop out of farrier school, and of course she can't go back to work until they heal," Keith said.

"And that could take months," Chloe finished.

"All right, what about her?" Mr. Sloane said, eyeing the kids suspiciously.

"We're organizing a ride to raise money for her,"

64

Megan said. "We're going to restage a Pony Express ride, all around Hickoryville."

"We've been getting people to sponsor us for however many miles we ride," Keith said.

"We've got a lot of money pledged already," Max said. "And we hope to have more by the time we ride, a week from Saturday."

"Well now, isn't that somethin'?" Mr. Sloane actually sounded impressed. "My Mandy's turned into a little fund-raiser. Next you'll be helpin' out Daddy's campaign, won't you, Sugar?" He took hold of Amanda's thin cheek and pinched it enthusiastically. Amanda broke loose with some effort, rubbing at her cheek.

Megan continued, "Well, Mr. Sloane, we were hoping that we could get you to agree to donate some money. In return, we'll tell people to vote for you for mayor."

Chloe added hastily, "Did you know that the fastest Pony Express ride ever was back in 1861, when the news of Abraham Lincoln's election was carried west by the Pony Express?"

Megan watched Mr. Sloane's scowling face intently. Gradually it relaxed into his version of a friendly smile. "Well now, I think that's honorable. Really. Y'all wantin' to help that poor girl. And I think it would be mighty good publicity for my campaign, if I were to be involved in it. Abraham Lincoln, you say? I tell you what. Here's what I'll do. I'll promise to match whatever amount of money you raise, under three conditions. First, you finish the ride. I can't stand nothin' done halfway."

"Oh, we're definitely going to finish," Megan assured him.

"Good. Number two. You make sure my name and my name only is connected with this event." He narrowed his eyes and glared at the children. "You didn't say nothin' about this to my opposin' candidate, did you?" When the children all swore that they hadn't, he said, "Good. See that you don't. I just want to see Rufus Lamar's face when he finds out I got the jump on him on this one!" The man chuckled as if he were enjoying a private joke.

"What's the third condition, Daddy?" Amanda prompted him.

"Why, only that my little Mandy rides in this Pony Express with y'all." He beamed at his daughter.

Amanda looked aghast. "Daddy, I can't!" she protested. "I don't ride nearly well enough to do somethin' like that! Tell him," she begged the other kids.

"Nonsense," Mr. Sloane said, before Megan could protest. His voice had taken on a tone of finality that any kid would recognize. "You will ride on this ride just like I said," Mr. Sloane declared. "Now run along," he ordered the kids. "I'm tryin' to take nap. I've got to make a speech this evenin' at the Civitan Club!"

Mr. Sloane crossed his arms, wiggled deeper into his recliner, and closed his eyes. A moment later he opened one eye again and saw five children still standing around him. "Go on!" Mr. Sloane snapped. He glared at the children until they had scurried out of the room.

Megan remembered the way to the front door. "Well, I guess that was a success," she said doubtfully.

"Oh, it was," Amanda assured her. "I haven't seen Daddy look so happy in months."

"That was happy?" Max said. "I'd hate to see him angry."

"You have no idea," Amanda told him.

Megan regarded Amanda sympathetically for a moment. It had to be hard to have parents like Mr. and Mrs. Sloane. Then they heard a car pull up outside. The car door slammed, and high-heeled shoes clicked purposefully toward the house.

"That's Mama," Amanda said.

"We'd better go," Megan said.

" 'Bye, Amanda," Chloe said.

"Are you sure you wouldn't like to stay for dinner?" Amanda asked hopefully.

From another section of the house came the sound of a door opening. "Mand-ee? Mandy Sue-ue!" Mrs. Sloane called.

"Um, I have tons of homework," Max said.

"Maybe some other time," Keith said.

"Well, g'bye," Amanda said politely.

"Amanda?" Mrs. Sloane's voice and footsteps were approaching.

"See you tomorrow," Megan said, reaching for the door handle. She pulled it open and the other kids rushed past her. Mr. Sloane had been scary enough. No one wanted to meet Mrs. Sloane on her own territory. "Oh," Megan added, pausing on her way out. "Don't worry about the ride," she said reassuringly to Amanda. "You'll be fine."

"I hope you're right," Amanda said. Megan saw a look of panic cross Amanda's face for a second. Then Mrs. Sloane's blond head appeared in the foyer, and Megan ducked out the door, pulling it firmly closed behind her.

She didn't see the other kids outside so she hurried down the steps and followed the stone walkway to the front gate. The four bicycles lay where they had left them just inside the gate, but the kids were nowhere in sight. At last Megan found them hiding behind a tall hedge covered with red pyracantha berries that bounded the Sloanes' front yard.

"Thanks for waiting for me," Megan said sarcastically.

"Well, Mrs. Sloane was coming. We didn't want to get stuck in there with her," Keith said.

"Neither did I," Megan said.

The kids spent the remaining days before the ride getting as many sponsors as they could. Mr. Sloane had had fliers printed to give to every person they spoke to. The fliers said in large red letters, "Gallop to the polls, and vote for Gerald R. Sloane for Mayor."

With Jules's help, they went over and over the map, memorizing the route around Hickoryville. Since Amanda had joined the group they had divided the ride into five sections, each one about fifteen miles long, beginning and ending at the town square in front of the courthouse.

"I want to have the first leg of the ride!" Keith announced.

"No, I want the first leg," Max said.

"Okay, then I'll take the last section," Keith offered.

"I want to be last!" Megan argued.

"They'll all be fun," Chloe reminded them.

"I don't want any of them," Amanda muttered.

"I tell you what," Jenny said. "You can draw for your routes."

Megan watched curiously as Jenny took five pieces of paper and numbered them one through five. Then she folded them and placed them in a riding helmet.

"Each slip of paper represents a leg of the ride. One is the first leg, and so on," Jenny explained. "Everybody draw one slip, and that will be your route. Fair enough?"

The kids agreed that it was. Jenny passed the hat, and each child drew a slip of paper. "Okay, one by one, open your slip and read me the number," Jenny said.

Max unfolded his paper. "One!" he said happily. That meant that Max would get to start the ride.

"Three," Keith read, sounding a little disappointed.

"That's the Natchez Trace leg," Jules reminded him.

"Okay, cool," Keith said, sounding a little happier.

"Girls?" Jenny prompted.

"Four," Amanda said worriedly. "Is four an easy route?"

"It's the shortest," Jules told her.

"Good," Amanda said with relief.

"But you have to go through the woods and up Thacker Mountain," Jules added.

"Oh," Amanda said, sounding terrified all over again.

Megan slowly opened her slip of paper. "Five, five, five!" she crowed. "I get to finish the ride!"

"That means Chloe has the second leg." Jenny finished writing down the names and numbers. "So, Max will start." The kids watched as she traced the routes on the map with her finger. "Then he'll pass the *mochila* to Chloe. Chloe hands it over to Keith, and Keith to Amanda. Amanda passes the *mochila* to Megan, who rides back into Hickoryville." Jenny's finger stabbed the tiny square at the center of town. "And the Pony Express lives again!"

The night before the ride, all the plans had been made. There was just one more thing the kids wanted to do. Children under thirteen weren't usually allowed in the hospital, but Megan and Max's mom let them in. They wanted to go visit Allie.

Dr. Morrison led them to the door of Allie's room. She knocked softly, then pushed the door open. "She's been waiting for you," she said.

Megan tiptoed in, Amanda, Chloe, Max, and Keith behind her. Allie sat propped up in the bed, her hands covered with thick bandages. "Hey, you rascals," she said happily. "Come over here where I can see you."

"Hi, Allie," Megan said. She was relieved to see Allie smiling.

"I sure have missed y'all," Allie said.

"We've missed you, too," Megan said.

"I didn't even realize how much a part of my life that ol' barn is," Allie said softly.

Megan heard the emotion in Allie's voice. "Well, you'll be back there soon," she told Allie confidently.

Allie shook her head. "I'm afraid not. The doctor says it'll be months before I can use my hands again for much of anything. I'm no good to the farm this way." She looked at her hands in disgust. "I can't even scratch my own nose, let alone a horse's."

"Well, we're going to help you, Allie," Keith said. "Right?"

"Right," Max said.

"Don't you worry, Allie," Chloe said. "Everybody helped me when my arm was broken, remember?"

"This is a sight worse than a broken arm," Allie said bitterly.

"Never mind," Megan said firmly. "We have a plan."

The kids had agreed to keep the ride a surprise, so they didn't tell her what the plan was. For a few more minutes they chatted with Allie, then Dr. Morrison came and herded them out. Before they left, Megan stuck her head around the door to wave at Allie one more time. But Allie's face was turned away. Megan saw a tear run down her cheek and splash onto one of her bandaged hands.

"We'll finish the ride," Megan said to herself. But for the first time since the group had planned the Pony Express ride, a finger of doubt began to poke at her heart. Could the Short Stirrup Club really do it? None of them had ever ridden fifteen miles cross-country. If they didn't finish, Mr. Sloane wouldn't put up his part of the money. And he'd insisted they include Amanda. Megan chewed at her lip. Amanda didn't even want to ride. What if she didn't try? What if she got lost? What if it got dark before Megan could make it back to town?

Megan watched Allie's shoulders shake with a quiet sob. "We'll make it," she said again to herself, more firmly. "I hope," she added under her breath. She pulled the door of Allie's room quietly closed and followed the others down the corridor.

# 7

WHEN MAX OPENED HIS EYES, THE BLUE NUMBERS ON his clock-radio seemed to float eerily in the darkness. 4:44? Why had he woken up so early? And why did he have that strange feeling in the pit of his stomach? It was the same feeling he got when he woke up Christmas morning, or before a horse show, or on the first day of school. The numbers changed. The clock read 4:45 and the radio began to play. Then Max remembered why he had set his alarm. Today was the day of the Pony Express!

He threw back the covers and turned on the lamp beside his bed. He'd chosen his clothes the night before, knowing it would be cold so early in the morning. Max put on warm socks, jeans, a T-shirt, a turtleneck, and a fleece pullover. After brushing his teeth, he went to wake up Megan.

In the kitchen, he found the Pop-Tarts and heated himself two. He started a pot of coffee for his parents, then downed the Pop-Tarts, along with a tall glass of milk. A moment later his sister came down the stairs, mute and sleepy. Max offered her a Pop-Tart but she shook her head and poured herself a glass of juice instead.

Soon James and Rose Morrison joined the children in the kitchen. "Thanks, son," James Morrison said, when he saw that Max had made the coffee.

"You're welcome," Max said, lacing up his paddock boots. When he had finished, he stood up and zipped his chaps. "Well, I'm all ready," he announced, tucking his safety helmet under one arm. "Come on, let's hit the road."

He watched, grinning, as Megan yawned hugely. "Usually you're the one rushing us," he noted, as his sister sleepily put on her coat and shuffled toward the door.

In the Bronco, Rose Morrison spoke. "Max, Megan, I want to tell you something," she began. "Since we moved to Hickoryville, you two have been involved in more schemes than I ever thought possible. But this is one I'm really proud of." She smiled warmly at her children, two deep dimples appearing in her pretty face.

Max smiled back at his mother. "Thanks, Mom," he said.

"Be careful out there," she couldn't help saying.

"We will, Mom," he assured her. Max didn't usually like unpredictable things. In horse shows he preferred the hunter divisions, where he and Popsicle could go slowly and methodically over simple fences in straight lines. "Safety Boy," his sister often called him, because he was always reminding the other kids to follow the rules. In about half an hour, Max was going to start a ride that would take him over fifteen miles of strange and varied terrain, beginning in the town and ending at a farmhouse somewhere out in the country. There would be plenty of unpredictable miles in that ride. But for some reason, Max felt oddly confident. He had been over and over the map of his route, and he was absolutely sure he would have nothing to worry about.

When the Morrisons pulled up in front of the courthouse, there was just a streak of red in the eastern sky. Quite a lot of people had turned out to watch the start of the ride. Most of them had pledged money to help Allie. They sat in their cars and pickup trucks, sipping coffee from thermoses and Styrofoam cups.

Max spotted the horse transport truck from Thistle Ridge Farm and waved to Jake, in the cab. Sharon, he knew, must be at the farm feeding the horses, since Jenny and Jules were going to help with the ride. Jules was just leading Popsicle down the ramp. The horse took funny, high steps because his legs were swathed in soft, bulky shipping wraps. At the bottom of the truck, Popsicle stopped. His head was up, and his ears pricked forward. He looked at his strange surroundings and let out a nervous snort, his breath escaping in two clouds of white steam.

From inside the trailer came a long, anxious whinny. It was Keith's horse, Penny, Popsicle's stablemate. Popsicle's head jerked toward the trailer as he let out a loud whinny in reply.

"Boy, he's a little 'up' this morning," Jules said, giving the lead shank a jerk. "Hey, be still there, Popsicle," she ordered him.

"It's okay, Popsicle," Max said, patting his horse's neck. He could feel the tension in the horse through his gloved hand. "It's okay, boy," he crooned, over and over. Popsicle stood still then and let Max pet him, but his eyes darted around, and his nostrils flared as he drew the cold air in and out.

In a few moments, Jenny had the horse tacked for Max. "I brought you something, Popsicle," Max said. From the pocket of his anorak, he took out something wrapped in paper. He unwrapped it and showed it to Popsicle. It was a cherry Popsicle!

"Look, boy, your favorite," Max said, offering the horse the frozen treat. Popsicle took a nervous nibble, then seemed to forget that he was in cold, strange surroundings. He slurped the Popsicle happily, red juice dripping from his mouth. When it was gone, he nosed at Max, hoping for more. "That's all I brought this morning," Max told his horse. "But I'll get you another one tonight when we're all finished," he promised.

The sky had turned the color of the cherry Popsicle. Jake surveyed it uneasily. "Red sky in the morning," he said, shaking his head.

"What do you mean, Jake?" Max said.

"Oh, nothin'," Jake said. "It's just an old wives' tale. It's supposed to mean a storm's comin', but I watched the weather report this mornin' and they didn't say anything about bad weather. I wouldn't worry about it."

But, Max noticed, Jake kept glancing uneasily at the dawn sky, as the red light spread across it from east to west.

"Want a leg up?" Jenny asked Max.

Max nodded. In spite of Jake's uneasiness, Max had never been more ready to ride. Jenny took hold of his left shin and boosted him into the saddle. Max found the stirrups and took up the reins, carefully untwisting them so that they ran in a flat, smooth line through his gloved hands. Jules led Popsicle through the growing crowd of people toward the front of the courthouse. "Where is everybody?" Max wondered aloud.

By everybody, Max meant Keith and Chloe and the Sloanes. Gerald Sloane was supposed to give a speech before Max rode off. But they were nowhere in sight. Max glanced at his watch. "It's almost six o'clock," he said. "They'd better get here soon."

Almost as soon as he said that, a long, shiny red

Lincoln turned onto the square and pulled up right in front of the courthouse. "There're the Sloanes," Jules said.

Gerald Sloane got out of the car, took his daughter by the wrist, and headed for the wooden platform set up for the mayoral candidates to give their speeches. Amanda stumbled along behind him. When Mr. Sloane reached the top of the platform, he took out a small megaphone and began to speak. "Friends," he began. "Ladies and gentlemen, fellow Americans . . ."

Mr. Sloane's voice faded from Max's ears. He was thinking of the book Chloe had lent him that told all about the Pony Express, and how it began over a hundred years ago. In his head, Max floated back in time to a small town known as "St. Jo," in the year 1860. Suddenly he was no longer Maxwell James Morrison, age eleven, of Hickoryville, Tennessee. He was handsome, twenty-year-old Johnny Fry, the best horseman in Kansas and the first rider on the first eastbound leg of the Pony Express.

It wasn't six A.M., it was six P.M., and Johnny was getting anxious. He'd been ready to leave since five; actually, he'd been ready to leave all day! He'd paced back and forth in the post office, his shining spurs jingling with every step, until he'd received word that the man bringing the mail from back east had missed his train, and would be delayed another hour.

Johnny's horse had been put on display then, to

amuse the impatient crowd. She was a fine bay mare, the fastest and strongest of his father's best stock. The people gathered around the horse, admiring the light saddle and the leather *mochila*. The *mochila* was really just a rectangle of leather, with a slit in front for the saddle horn, and another slit for the cantle in back. Four locking rectangular leather pouches were sewn onto the corners to hold the mail. The *mochila* had been specially designed for the Pony Express by a Missouri saddle maker named Israel Landis. Soon, Johnny thought, he would be putting it to the test.

Then a bored spectator decided to take a souvenir. He plucked a shining black hair from the bay mare's tail. Others joined in. By the time Johnny angrily shooed the people away, the little mare had stood bravely while her tail was plucked nearly bare.

Johnny was glad when the train whistle sounded the arrival of the mail courier. He waited impatiently while speeches were made. The mail, written on special oiled silk to keep it light and protect it from the weather, was inserted into the pouches on the *mochila*. Then, with great fanfare and cheering crowds, Johnny leaped lightly into the saddle and pounded away, as eager as his tailless mare. As he flashed by, a pretty girl reached out and playfully grabbed at his fancy embroidered shirt, tearing off a scrap of it. She sewed the scrap into a quilt and passed it on to her children, and they to their children. The little scrap of cloth was a piece of history.

Back in Hickoryville, at six A.M., Max Morrison looked into the red sky and got ready to make history all over again. Popsicle was ready, too. The quiet gelding, usually calm and laid back, pranced and jigged in the frosty morning air, though Jules held him firmly by the reins.

The growing crowd murmured and pointed at the horse and rider. It seemed that the whole town of Hickoryville had gathered to see the beginning of the first Pony Express ride of the twentieth century. People who worked on Saturday stood dressed in their suits and ties. Mothers and fathers stood with their children. Gerald Sloane finished his speech, and the people who had been listening applauded politely.

"Now, my daughter, Amanda Susannah Sloane, will place this important message in the mailbag yonder," Gerald Sloane said, pointing at Max. Max glanced down at the *mochila*. He and the other kids had made it from an old pair of chaps with broken zippers, and a couple of old leather purses they'd found at a thrift shop. "And our first Pony Express rider will be off!"

The crowd cheered as Mr. Sloane gave Amanda a little shove toward the platform steps. "And remember," Mr. Sloane added, as Amanda made her way toward Max, "the contents of this envelope are very important. The riders must complete their run and be back here by six o'clock this evenin', when I will announce the important message in the envelope. And if they do complete it, in the allotted time, I will personally match whatever money they have raised from your generous donations!" Gerald Sloane declared.

The crowd responded again with applause. "And don't forget," Mr. Sloane went on, "my daughter, Amanda Sloane, will personally be riding on the most grueling leg of the run." Max watched Mr. Sloane beam at Amanda, who looked as if she might throw up. "As you know, the Sloanes have always been known for their generosity and community spirit." Mr. Sloane surveyed the crowd. "I don't believe I see my opposing candidate, Rufus Lamar, present this mornin'," he observed. "Or his son, who ought to be out there participatin' in this ride, like my own daughter."

Some people showed their appreciation with cheers and whistles. Amanda inserted the envelope into one of the pouches on the *mochila*. "You look real nice, Max," she said, smiling encouragingly at him.

"Have you seen the others?" Max asked her.

Amanda shook her head. Max scanned the crowd, looking for his sister, Keith, and Chloe. He spotted his parents and waved. Then he felt a tug at his chaps. Was a spectator trying to rip off a piece of them?

"Max!" Keith said, tugging on his chaps again to get his attention.

"Keith!" Max said, relieved to see his friend. Megan and Chloe were making their way through the crowd. "Where have you guys been?" he demanded, when they were all by his side.

"Mamaw's car wouldn't start this morning," Chloe explained. "I'm sorry I'm late."

"I was over there with Jake," Keith said. "Didn't you see me?"

"No," Max said. "I thought you guys weren't going to show."

"We wouldn't do that!" Keith exclaimed.

"Come on, it's time," Megan said. "Let's do our cheer for good luck."

"Max, wait—your helmet!" Chloe was pointing to Max's bare heard. Somehow, in all the commotion, he had forgotten to put it on. Chloe volunteered to go and find it for him.

"Hey, where'd you get the spurs?" Keith said, pointing at Max's feet.

"Spurs?" Megan said doubtfully. Max had strapped on a pair of rather long spurs over his paddock boots. "What are you wearing those for?" Megan asked, pointing to them.

Max had borrowed the spurs from Rufus Lamar's son, Tyler, a bigger boy who rode at Thistle Ridge. Max himself had never worn spurs. Popsicle was slow sometimes, but Max liked him that way. And he could usually get the horse going with a smack from his bat. Spurs, he knew, were for times when a rider needed extra responsiveness from his horse. Sharon always said a rider wasn't ready to wear a spur until he could keep his leg still and make the horse do anything he wanted *without* a spur. "The thing about wearing spurs is not knowing when to use them, but knowing when *not* to use them. Anyway, if you can make your horse listen without a spur, what do you need to wear them for?" she would point out. Max pushed the thought out of his head. He liked how the silvery spurs flashed cunningly in the morning light. They made him feel powerful. "Johnny Fry wore spurs," Max said defensively.

"Who's Johnny Fry?" Megan asked, as Chloe returned with Max's safety helmet.

"Never mind," Max said. He put on the helmet and fastened it. "I'm ready," he announced.

Megan, Keith, Chloe, and Amanda piled their hands one on top of the other. Max leaned over and put his hand on top. "Short Stirrup Club!" they cheered.

"For Allie," Max added under his breath.

Jules let go of Popsicle's reins. "Go get 'em, kid," she said.

"I'll be ready at the next station," Chloe called to Max.

But Max Johnny Fry Morrison didn't hear her. He was already heading down Lamar Street, the courthouse and the crowds fading into memory behind him as he rode out of town.

Max had meant to gallop. He had pictured himself thundering down Lamar, just like Johnny Fry had galloped out of St. Jo. He had even started out with a few strides of canter. But then Max realized that the asphalt was slippery under his horse's metal shoes. He proceeded at a cautious, awkward trot instead, threading his way down the street, which had been closed to traffic by police cars for the occasion. Some of the officers waved to him as he trotted by.

Popsicle's hooves clopped loudly on the street, echoing through the quiet town. The horse's neck was arched, and his ears flicked nervously forward and back as they trotted along. For the first time Max could ever remember, he actually had to hold Popsicle back. He had already begun to regret putting on the spurs. He held his toes in, sensing that if Popsicle felt a spur he would probably explode into a gallop. Max was relieved when he turned onto Barr Street. A few minutes later he stepped off the road and allowed Popsicle to canter. Then it was easy to imagine that he really was Johnny Fry, as he and Popsicle cantered across somebody's cornfield that had been plowed under for the winter.

Popsicle seemed to relax as they cantered along. Soon they crossed the cornfield and headed across a stretch of pasture. In the soft, pink light, frost covered everything, decorating the dry grasses and the empty limbs of the trees. Max had time to notice how beautiful everything was in the very early morning; there was a special quality to the light that he had never seen at another time of day. Then the first real rays of sun touched the frost, scattering the whiteness into a zillion tiny sparkles of red and blue and gold. In the next few minutes, the sun bounded into the blue overhead, chasing away the few clouds that had haunted the morning sky. Max was glad that in spite of Jake's warning about the weather, the day had begun as clear and calm as could be.

Soon Popsicle let out a snort and lowered his head. Max listened to the horse's breathing, letting him canter until he started to sound tired. Then he slowed Popsicle to a medium trot and posted along, enjoying the ride.

It was different and exciting to be riding all alone through strange pastures. With the county road on his left to guide him, Max trotted along. Popsicle had settled into a comfortable, swinging stride that seemed to eat up the miles. Occasionally a car or truck passed by on the road. The driver would almost always wave or toot the horn in a friendly salute. Max waved back, feeling very important.

Then he saw the Thistle Ridge horse van pass by. Max waved enthusiastically and gave them the thumbs-up. So far, the first leg of the journey was going great. He was almost sad when, after an hour and a half, the farmhouse that marked the end of his route was in sight.

He had been walking for five minutes or so, letting Popsicle rest. Max leaned forward and watched Popsicle's nostrils for a moment. The horse was breathing normally. Max looked up at the farmhouse and saw Chloe and Jump For Joy standing ready. His leg of the ride was over, but Max decided to end it with a bang.

The other kids, especially Megan, always teased him about being so cautious. Max had only fallen off Popsicle once in his whole life. And only once had he ever really galloped. He eyed the farmhouse, which sat at the top of a long, sloping hill. Then Max made up his mind, and a little thrill raced through his middle. He would show them; he would cut loose like they never imagined! He would gallop the last stretch up that hill and come roaring in, just like Johnny Fry must have ridden into his last stop on the real Pony Express all those years ago. Max gathered up the reins and leaned forward, anticipating the feel of the gallop. One well-aimed kick of his heels and he would fly! But Max had forgotten one thing; he was wearing spurs.

# 8

CHLOE GOODMAN STOOD IN FRONT OF THE FARMHOUSE, watching anxiously for Max. Megan stood beside her. When they saw Max ride into view, Chloe waved enthusiastically. "There he is!" she said excitedly. "There's Max!"

"Why's Popsicle walking?" Megan said. "This is supposed to be the Pony *Express.*"

"He's probably just resting," Keith observed. "You can't gallop the whole time, you know," he cautioned her.

"Hey, it looks like Safety Boy is actually going to canter!" Megan said. "Look!" She made her voice low and intense, like a sports announcer. "He's shortening up the reins," she chanted. "He's getting into two-point position. He's waving to the spectators as he prepares to dazzle us with a few strides of canter, and he's—off?" Megan's commentary turned into a question as her brother spurred his horse and then flew—right out of the saddle!

"Uh-oh," Chloe said in amazement, as she saw Popsicle throw his hindquarters skyward in the biggest buck the kids had even seen. Max sailed over the horse's head in a perfect arc, landing on his seat in a mud puddle crusted with thin ice.

"Wow!" Keith exclaimed in awe.

Megan collapsed into hysterical laughter.

"Oh, no, I hope he's all right," Chloe said, biting her bottom lip.

Popsicle charged up the hill, riderless. He galloped right up to Jump For Joy, and the horse and pony touched noses, blowing air into each other's nostrils in greeting. Jules caught Popsicle, as Max limped the rest of the way up the hill.

"Are you okay?" Chloe asked him. Max's cheeks were bright red. Whether it was from the chilly air or from embarrassment, Chloe couldn't tell.

"I'm fine," Max said.

"What happened down there?" Chloe asked him. "I never saw Popsicle buck like that, ever."

"And you never will again," Max promised. "I wanted to end my ride with a splash—"

"You ended with a splash all right," Megan interrupted. "Right in a mud puddle!" Still laughing, she pointed to Max's soaking, muddy chaps.

"Thanks for pointing that out to me, Megan," Max said sarcastically. He bent and unbuckled Tyler's spurs and stood up, holding the dripping spurs before him. "I don't think I'll be needing these anymore," he said sheepishly. "I'm sorry, Popsicle," Max told his horse sincerely.

Just then Popsicle let out a snort, as if he thoroughly agreed. The kids all laughed.

"Hey, I thought the Pony Express had only two minutes to change riders," Jenny reminded them. "You'd better get a move on, Chloe," she said, imitating the gravelly drawl of an old cowpoke. "You're burnin' daylight."

Max lifted the *mochila* from his saddle and gave it to Chloe, who placed it over her own saddle. Then Jenny gave her a leg up on her little white pony, Jump For Joy.

"Ready?" Jenny asked.

Chloe nodded firmly, but her hands shook as she adjusted the reins. Max had seemed so calm and collected when he'd ridden out of Hickoryville. Chloe felt completely the opposite. She was having trouble getting a deep breath, and even her legs were trembling. The thought of riding all those miles all by herself was daunting.

But she put on a brave face and turned Jump For Joy down the hill behind the farmhouse, heading into the next leg of the ride. "Keep thinking of Allie," she told herself firmly, to keep her courage up. She gave the pony his head and let him pick his own way carefully down the hill. When she reached the bottom of the hill, she turned and looked back. She saw Megan waving to her. She waved back, then looked forward toward the wide stretch of bottom land she had to cross and, drawing a shaky breath, picked up a canter.

Jump For Joy's canter was smooth and steady. Chloe stayed in a light seat, keeping most of her weight down in her legs and heels. That was the best position for riding cross-country for long stretches, she knew. It would keep both her pony's back and her own seat from getting too tired.

They crossed the bottom and started up a gently sloping hill. Chloe pulled her pony back to a trot. At the crest of the hill she caught a glimpse of the town of Hickoryville on her right. Here and there its streets and houses peeked through the trees. She let Jump For Joy walk down the hill and trotted on, but soon she had to let him walk again. She was crossing somebody's cotton field that had been picked over. The gray stalks of the cotton plants clung with thin, stingy claws to the drooping white bolls the picker had left behind. They scratched at Chloe's legs with skeleton fingers as she rode down a row, and seemed to grab at Jump For Joy's shining, silky tail.

Then she thought she heard something, a rustling in the cotton field a few rows over. She stopped, listening intently, but didn't hear it again. Jump For Joy stomped impatiently and tossed his white head. His creamy mane flashed in the sunlight. "It's probably just a rabbit or a squirrel,"

Chloe said to reassure herself. She rode on. Chloe didn't like the cotton fields after they had been picked. They reminded her of worn-out, sad things, like the drab hand-me-downs she received from her older cousins.

She was glad when she'd threaded her way down the long row and come out at the other side of the cotton field. Jump For Joy seemed glad, too. He picked up a trot, shaking his head as if to rid himself of the feel of the prickly cotton stalks. He swished his tail back and forth. Chloe glanced back and saw that a broken piece of a cotton stalk with a few bolls attached still clung to his tail. At last he shook it free. They trotted on toward a pasture, leaving the cotton field behind them.

As they approached the pasture, Chloe noticed that it was surrounded by a barbed wire fence. She rode along it, looking for a gap. At last she spotted a gravel road that crossed the fence line. There was a cattle guard across it. The cattle guard was like a bridge made of long strips of metal that ran crosswise on the ground. They were set about five or six inches apart, over a ditch a couple of feet deep. If a cow tried to cross it, its foot would slip through the gaps between the metal strips. So would a horse's. Horses and cows just seemed to know this; they never tried to cross a cattle guard.

Chloe halted before the cattle guard and stood, trying to figure out how she could get across. She knew this pasture. It belonged to Mr. Allen, who owned Briar Creek Farm, just down the road from Thistle Ridge. The cattle guard looked new, she noticed. It must have just been installed. The dirt that had been dug up around it was moist and darker red than the road.

"Shoot!" Chloe said aloud. "There was supposed to be a gate here. How're we supposed to get across this cattle guard?"

She turned the pony to the side and trotted along the fenceline, searching once more for a gap in the barbed wire. She found none. Sighing, she rode back to the cattle guard. What could she do? Go around the pasture? She remembered from Jake's map that there was a deep ravine on one side. She couldn't ride through that. And if she went around the other side, she would lose too much time.

Could she jump the barbed wire fence? Chloe eyed it doubtfully. She knew it was dangerous to jump barbed wire. A horse might not see the thin strands, and could hang his legs in it trying to jump it. Besides, the top strand was nearly four feet high. Chloe had never jumped more than two feet. And Jump For Joy had just started over small jumps again, after spending most of the summer recovering from a torn suspensory ligament. Chloe didn't dare risk injuring the leg again.

She eyed the cattle guard. It was about three feet wide, but at least it was flat. She didn't like the idea, but she guessed she would just have to jump over it.

Chloe walked several feet away to get an approach and stopped again, facing the cattle guard. She licked her lips. "Okay, pony," she said to Jump For Joy. "We're going to jump this thing. Ready?" She shortened the reins and pressed the pony's sides with her legs.

Jump For Joy trotted willingly toward the cattle guard. Chloe got into jumping position and grabbed a handful of mane, so she'd be sure not to yank him in the mouth if he jumped big. A couple of feet from the cattle guard, the pony dropped his head, as if he were taking a good look at the obstacle. Chloe prepared to feel the pony take off.

A second later, she was glad she was holding the mane. Jump For Joy planted his front legs and skidded to a stop!

Chloe landed on the pony's withers, in front of the saddle. Quickly she scooted herself back into the saddle, laughing nervously. "Pony!" she scolded him. "You're not supposed to stop like that."

She turned him around and trotted away again. Then she approached the cattle guard, this time at a canter. She clucked encouragingly at him, sure that this time he would jump it. But again he refused.

Chloe was getting really nervous. "Pony, we have to get over this cattle guard," she pleaded. "Please?" She tried the approach one more time. Again, at the last second, she felt the pony hesitate. She dug her legs into his sides and made a clucking sound to encourage him. To her relief, she felt him surge forward again. She grabbed mane and got ready to feel the jump.

Chloe must have closed her eyes, because a second later she had to make herself open them. She was standing in her stirrups in two-point position, clutching her pony's mane. But he hadn't jumped. He was crossing the cattle guard, very carefully placing his feet one after another on the three-inch metal strips. Chloe held her breath, sure he would step between them and injure a leg. But to her amazement he picked his way nimbly across the last few strips and scampered away, snorting as if he were extremely proud of himself.

Chloe leaned forward and hugged him affectionately. "You are the smartest pony in the whole world!" she declared. "Wait until the other kids hear how you walked across the cattle guard!" Laughing with relief, she cantered toward the hill before her.

She followed the dirt road to the other side of the pasture and was glad to see an ordinary metal gate. She dismounted, led Jump For Joy through the gate, then closed it carefully behind her. As she was mounting up again, something caught her eye—a shape or a shadow that moved in a row of cedar trees at the edge of the pasture. Chloe peered anxiously at the spot where it had been, but saw only waving grasses. With a strange, prickly feeling at the back of her neck, she trotted on. Was someone following her?

Soon Chloe came to the creek that marked the last stretch of her run. In the spring, runoff water from a bigger creek coursed through the creek bed, but for months now it had been dried up. The banks of the creek were steeper than she had imagined. Chloe found a spot that didn't look too slippery and, leaning way back, pointed her pony at the steep bank. Jump For Joy braced his front legs and nearly sat down on his haunches, sliding down the bank into the sandy creek bed.

"That was kind of fun," Chloe said, patting the pony's neck. She aimed him upcreek. "Okay, we're almost there." She checked her watch and noticed with dismay that she was about ten minutes behind schedule. The delay at the cattle guard had set her back. She pressed Jump For Joy into a brisk trot along the flat creek bed, hoping to make up the lost time.

Suddenly Jump For Joy's head snapped up and his regular rhythm faltered. He began to walk. Chloe urged him on, clucking at him, but he ignored her commands and continued walking. His head turned nervously left and right, as if he were confused, or searching for something.

"What's the matter, pony?" Chloe asked uneasily. She wished he could tell her. Sometimes she swore he could understand her words, but try as she might, she couldn't read the pony's thoughts.

Abruptly Jump For Joy stopped. Chloe felt the hair on the back of her neck rise. She had the distinct feeling that someone, or something, was watching her. She looked around her carefully, searching for whoever or whatever it was. "Hello?" she called out tentatively.

Then Jump For Joy wheeled around, and Chloe gasped. Standing in the creek bed, not twenty feet away from her, was a big, shaggy, wild-looking dog.

"Oh, poor thing," Chloe said softly. She was glad it was just a dog. Chloe was used to taming strays. They seemed to seek her out, knowing she had a soft spot for homeless animals. "Are you lost?" she asked it. "Come here." She whistled softly, patting her thigh.

The dog lowered its head, its eyes fixed not on Chloe, but upon her pony. Chloe felt Jump For Joy's whole body tense, as the dog took a step toward them.

*Not a dog*, Chloe realized. Her heart began to pound as she sensed she was in danger. It was not a dog that faced them, its yellow eyes glaring with menace. The creature let its jaw drop open, and Chloe saw the gleam of a white fang. She knew this animal. She knew they roamed the hills in this area, but that usually they kept away from people—unless they were hungry. "Coyote," Chloe whispered.

Then everything happened at once. The coyote

silently sprang forward. Jump For Joy spun on his haunches and galloped up the creek bed, his small hooves digging hard into the sandy footing.

Chloe could hardly breathe, she was so frightened. She bent low over the pony's neck. "Run," she begged him, but he needed no encouragement. Branches whipped by, and sand flew from the pony's feet as he twisted left and right, following the bends in the creek.

Would the coyote follow them? Chloe made herself look back over her shoulder. She didn't see him. She let Jump For Joy canter on for another minute, then the branches grew lower as the creek bed rose higher. Soon she could see over the bank. She would have to get out of the creek, or the low branches would scrape her off. Ducking another branch, she slowed to a trot, and turned Jump For Joy toward the bank, feeling his hindquarters dig in as they rode up and out of the creek bed.

Had the coyote followed? Chloe looked back once more and felt her heart turn colder than the chilly air as the coyote's shaggy gray head appeared at the top of the bank, just a few feet away.

Chloe clamped her legs around Jump For Joy's sides and pushed the reins toward his head. The pony tore across the field, his white mane stinging Chloe's cheeks. It was hard to keep her eyes open. Squinting, Chloe saw the green and black van from Thistle Ridge up ahead, in the parking lot of the Natchez Trace Visitors' Center. She glanced over her shoulder and to her horror saw that the coyote had closed the distance between them. She saw his yellow eyes glinting and his teeth bared as he lunged at her pony's heels.

"Nooo!" she screamed. "Go away! You leave my pony alone!"

Then suddenly, a black-and-white blur blazed toward her from the parking lot up ahead. Chloe recognized Merlin, Jake's border collie. The dog tore past her at lightning speed to go after the coyote. Chloe saw the coyote falter and break away. Merlin chased after him until he slunk into the grass and vanished, headed back toward the creek bed. When he was satisfied that the coyote was gone, the border collie came trotting back, a pleased expression on his face.

Chloe pulled Jump For Joy back to a trot and made it the last few feet to the parking lot. Then she slid off his back, trembling.

"Chloe, are you all right?" Megan asked anxiously.

"Did you see that?" Chloe asked shakily.

Jake came running up. "Chloe, what was it?" Jake asked her. "Was something chasing you?"

Chloe nodded, panting. "A coyote. It was following us for a while." Chloe shuddered, thinking of the rustle in the cotton field. The coyote had been very close to them. "It chased us all the way through the creek bed."

"It's unusual for a coyote to be out during the

day," Jake said. "They're night hunters. It must have been sick, or very hungry."

Merlin trotted up and shoved his cold, wet nose into Chloe's hand. Chloe knelt and hugged the dog. "Merlin, you saved us! That ol' coyote nearly had us! If it hadn't been for you, there's no telling what would have happened."

"Merlin saves the day! Again," Max said, reminding them how the smart, brave border collie had helped his human friends out before.

Jules came forward and took the reins from Chloe. "Give me that pony," she said. "He needs walking out."

Max pulled the *mochila* from the pony's back, while Megan ran up the stirrups and loosened the girth. Jenny threw a wool cooler over Jump For Joy and began leading him around.

Chloe simply stood, waiting for her racing heart to slow down and her breathing to return to normal. She watched Jump For Joy walking around the parking lot with Jules. Then, just when she thought everything would be all right, she saw something strange in the pony's gait. She felt her eyes blur with tears as she realized the unthinkable: Jump For Joy was limping.

# 9

"LOOK AT JUMP FOR JOY," KEITH SAID, POINTING TO THE little white pony.

"It looks like his left front," Jenny remarked, as she smoothed the *mochila* and gave Keith a leg up.

"That's the same leg he hurt before," Keith said. He remembered how the pony had spent weeks on stall rest, while they waited for his leg to heal.

"I hope he didn't reinjure the tendon," Jenny said worriedly.

Keith hoped so, too. He felt bad for Chloe. He reached forward and patted his chestnut mare's soft neck. What if something happened to Penny? Keith had been looking forward to this ride, even if he hadn't gotten to be the first rider. But he had begun to worry. Already Max had fallen off, and

Chloe had been chased by a coyote. What would happen next?

Keith and the other kids watched as Jules expertly ran her hands down Jump For Joy's legs, feeling for heat or swelling. "I don't feel anything unusual," she said. She led the pony a few steps forward. He was still obviously favoring his left front leg, even at the walk. Suddenly Jules bent and picked up the pony's foot. A second later she set his foot down and led him forward again. This time he walked normally.

"There. All fixed," Jules said.

"What was it? How come he's not limping anymore?" Megan asked.

"I know," Keith said. "A rock was in his foot."

Jules held up a rough rock, the size of a shooter marble. "You'd limp, too, if this was digging into your foot," she said.

"Oh, I'm so glad," Chloe said, hugging her pony's neck. Then she hugged Jules. "Thank you, Jules," Chloe said.

Keith was relieved that Jump For Joy wasn't lame. Maybe everything would be okay after all. "Ready, old girl?" he asked his mare.

Penny, Keith's horse, simply stood patiently. She was old and dependable. Penny would stand and face a freight train, until she was asked to move.

"Is your cinch tight?" Max asked Keith.

"Yep," Keith said, grinning. He had a long history of falling off because he had failed to tighten the cinch on his western saddle. Penny would be jogging along, and suddenly the saddle would slip to the side, dumping Keith to the ground. "She doesn't puff up her belly now that she's pregnant," Keith explained.

Jenny checked it anyway, just to be sure, but she couldn't get it any tighter. "Okay, I guess you're in good shape," she said, giving the mare an affectionate pat on the shoulder.

"How am I doing on time?" Keith asked.

"You're just a little behind schedule, the way we figured it," Jenny told him. "As long as we don't have bad weather, you guys should still finish up on time, no problem."

Keith glanced at the sky. A few clouds were gathering in the northwest, but they seemed far away, and there was no wind to blow them closer. "Well, here I go," Keith announced. He waved good-bye, shifted the reins to turn Penny, and started for the trial at a jog.

Keith knew all about the Natchez Trace. His father, who was an archaeologist, had told him how the early settlers had walked across the hills and woods and plains from East to West, their feet pounding out trails over the land. Indians had used the trails, too.

The real Natchez Trace was a road from Natchez, Mississippi, to Nashville, Tennessee. Now, of course, there was a highway there. But parts of the old Natchez Trace still remained, including this section around Hickoryville.

Keith and Penny jogged along the trail, which was about as wide as a single-lane road. It ran through a pine wood, and layer upon layer of brown needles had fallen upon the trail, making a quiet, springy path for Penny's feet. The clean, evergreen scent of the pines mixed with the earthier smell of the fallen needles and the bark of their trunks. Keith breathed deeply, enjoying the smell.

Jogging through the pine woods on a section of the real Natchez Trace made Keith remember his ancestors. His mind wandered back to the days when Indians had roamed this land: Choctaw and Chickasaw. He glimpsed clearings in the woods and imagined their tipis standing there. Small secret paths wound through the trees where moccasined feet had once padded silently, searching for game.

In the trail beneath his horse's feet, in the pine woods around him, in the fragments of sky overhead, Keith felt the spirit of the people who had once lived and traveled along this trail. It would have been wrong to shout here, he thought. Or to break off a tree branch, or stray from the Trace. It was a sacred place: a place to hush, Keith thought, and to listen to the heart. He rode along, full of the same solemn reverence he felt whenever he entered a church.

He had been going for about an hour, enjoying

the ride, when a sound roared through the silent woods. Keith jerked in fright and felt Penny shy. She bolted for five strides before she remembered her manners and returned to her rhythmic jog.

Keith's heart was thumping from the scare. But he knew what the sound was. His ears still rang in protest at the terrible noise. It was a gunshot.

He looked around uneasily. The gun had sounded awfully close. Was someone hunting in these woods? He knew it was deer season, but hunting on the Natchez Trace was against the law.

Keith wanted to get far away from the place where he'd heard the gunshot. He nudged Penny with his right leg, shifted his seat, and she broke into a lope. After just a few minutes, though, Penny was huffing and puffing and needed a rest. He let her walk, looking and listening anxiously all around him for any signs of hunters.

Then, with a crackling of brush and branches, a deer leaped onto the trace in front of him. Penny stopped. So did the deer. It seemed surprised to see a boy and a horse in its path. It was a big, sturdy buck, with a rack of antlers. Its gray coat lay smoothly over taut muscles. Keith gazed into the buck's dark eyes and saw no fear there, only a curious regard. Keith was keenly aware that he was a visitor in the deer's world. He watched the majestic animal reverently. The buck's sensitive nose moved, sampling the air. Keith had time to count ten points on each regal antler before the quiet woods again exploded with gunshot.

As quickly as the buck had appeared, it bounded away. Keith glimpsed the buck's white tail raised in a flag of warning before it vanished into the woods. But then another shot cracked through the still air, splitting pine bark on a tree dangerously close to Keith and Penny.

For one second Keith froze. He stared at the tree, its creamy insides oozing yellow pine sap where the bullet had struck. Then he woke up, clamped his legs around Penny's sides, and sent her into a gallop.

"Go, Penny!" Keith said. The old mare flew down the trail like a much younger horse. Keith was scared to death. He knew the hunters must be after the buck, but he was afraid if they saw Penny, they might shoot at her. Through the sights of a gun, the brown rump of a horse might look a lot like the haunches of a deer.

Keith and Penny sped down the old trail. Then suddenly, to Keith's surprise, Penny plunged to the right, off the trail, and headed into the pine woods.

"Hey!" he cried out. He shifted the reins to the left, and with a thump from his right leg tried to turn her around. Penny took one stride toward the left, but then headed back in the direction she'd been going.

"Penny!" Keith said, pulling firmly on the reins. He couldn't imagine why she had suddenly bolted into the woods with him, but he knew they were nearly at the end of his run. Jake and the others would be waiting for him at the end of the Trace. This was no time to go off on an excursion through the woods, especially if there were hunters around.

But Penny wouldn't stop. She plowed on through the pine woods. More than once, Keith had to duck to avoid getting whacked in the head by a low branch. Suddenly another shot boomed through the woods, and a bullet ripped through the branches on his left.

Keith cried out in panic. Once more he tried to stop Penny, or turn her back toward the Trace. At least if he was on the open Trace, they'd be less likely to be taken for a deer.

Then Keith heard someone shout. Was it the hunters? "Hey!" he screamed. "It's me! Don't shoot, please!"

"Keith?" someone called. "Keith, where are you?"

Through a small clearing in the trees, Keith saw Jake. At the same time, Penny slowed to a jog, then a walk. "Jake!" Keith said, feeling relief flood through him.

Jake hurried over to him. "Are you okay, son?" His forehead was creased with worry as he looked Keith over.

Keith nodded. He told Jake how the hunters had been shooting terribly close to him and Penny. "Then Penny started running through the woods, off the Trace, and I couldn't get her to turn back." Keith's story tumbled out of him. "Man, am I glad to see you, Jake."

"It's a good thing Penny turned off the path," Jake told him. "When we got to the parking lot down there at the end of the Trace, the park rangers were there. They've been trying to catch these people hunting illegally for a couple of weeks. When I found out there were poachers out here, I went looking for you, to bring you around this way. Penny saved you, son. If you had kept going down the trace that way, you would have run right into those hunters. Somehow she must have known they were up there. That's one smart little ol' mare you got there," Jake said appreciatively.

"She sure is," Keith said, giving Penny a loving hug. "Thanks, Penny."

A second later the woods thinned out, and Keith and Jake walked into the parking lot where the horse van was parked. Max, Megan, and Chloe rushed up to meet them.

"Keith, are you okay? We heard all these gunshots, and we were so scared! We thought you might get shot. Did you see the hunters? Are you sure you're all right?" The kids' questions tumbled out faster than Keith could answer them.

"Thanks to Penny, we're just fine," Keith assured the others.

"All right," Max said. "High five." He stuck his hand out toward Keith.

Keith leaned over to slap Max's hand. When he did, his saddle slid sideways, dumping him off his horse.

"Yep," Keith said. "We're perfectly fine." He sat in the parking lot, looking lovingly up at his horse, while everyone laughed.

# 10

AMANDA LAUGHED WITH THE OTHERS WHEN KEITH'S saddle slipped. But it was a high-pitched, nervous laugh, and she wasn't really enjoying herself. Amanda was petrified.

She had spent the whole summer and fall trying to impress the other kids, so that they would include her in the Short Stirrup Club. No matter how hard she tried, nothing had worked. To her amazement, when she had finally found the courage to just ask, the other kids had welcomed her into the club. Amanda had been delighted to feel like part of the group, although she was still figuring out what they expected from her.

One thing she had learned about the Short Stirrup Club was that they spent a lot of time riding their horses together. Amanda had only recently decided that she actually *liked* her big appendix quarter horse, Prince Charming. But liking the horse and liking *riding* the horse were two entirely different things. Amanda had fallen off Prince Charming more times than she could count.

While she was glad to help out with the Short Stirrup Club's fund-raising, she had absolutely no wish to ride in the Pony Express. She had tried to tell her father she didn't want to ride, but he had refused to listen, as usual. He was so caught up in his campaign for mayor that he couldn't pay attention to anything else.

So once again, Amanda was stuck doing something other people had forced on her without considering her wishes. She stood holding Prince Charming, waiting anxiously for someone to put on the *mochila* and give her a leg up.

Jenny had taken the *mochila* from Penny's saddle. She carried it over and set it on Amanda's expensive Hermès saddle. After tightening the girth, she looked at Amanda. "How're you doing there, Amanda?" she asked. "Ready to mount up?"

Amanda could only nod. Her voice felt stuck in her throat.

"Okay then," Jenny said. "Let's get you up there."

Amanda turned around, her knees quaking, and faced the saddle. It seemed miles above her. She took the reins in her left hand, grabbed mane, and put her right hand on the pommel.

"One, two, three," Jenny said, and hoisted her saddleward.

When she hit the saddle, Amanda thought she might faint. Then she actively wished she would. She was dressed warmly, but her whole body was shaking. Her fear was a cold lump in her stomach that was slowly rising, filling her up inside. She glanced up at the sky. A hazy film of cloud cover had begun to form a pastel wash over the sun. Amanda stared wordlessly at the other kids, who had come over to wish her well.

"Don't worry, Amanda," Megan said. "You'll be fine. Just follow the trail." She pointed at the hiking trail that was supposed to take Amanda through the woods, over Thacker Mountain, which was really just a very high hill, and down to the lake on the other side. There the others would be waiting for her.

Amanda had been over the route a thousand times on the map. But it didn't make her feel any less afraid. What if she fell off? What if she got lost? What if no one found her and she had to spend the night alone in the woods? She opened her mouth then. She was going to tell them she couldn't do it, that she was simply too afraid.

But she couldn't say it. They were all counting on her—Megan, Max, Chloe, and Keith. She had made such a big deal about wanting to be in the Short Stirrup Club, now that she was in it, she couldn't quit on them. They'd never forgive her.

Her father would be disappointed in her. And then there was Allie. Amanda had been shocked to see Allie looking so sad and hurt in the hospital. If Amanda didn't ride, her dad wouldn't donate the rest of the money for Allie. How could she back out?

Amanda took a deep breath and tried to focus on the whole picture. It helped a little. Her fear seemed smaller compared to the idea of letting everyone down. And a little tiny voice inside her whispered, *It's time you tested yourself, Amanda. If you don't learn to ride this horse now, you never will. Just follow the trail.*

"Just follow the trail," Amanda whispered fiercely.

"What?" Megan asked.

"Nothing," Amanda said. At least she had her voice back.

"Amanda," Jenny said, "you can do this."

Amanda looked at Jenny's warm eyes. A light of encouragement seemed to radiate from them. Amanda felt it thawing the cold lump of fear inside her. "I can do this," she repeated.

"Stay on the trail, and trot and canter as much as you can," Jules told her. "Your route is the shortest, but it's getting late, and it's clouding over," she said, glancing anxiously at the sky. "That means it's going to get dark earlier than we expected. So try and keep your pace up."

"Keep the pace up," Amanda repeated. She was

beginning to feel like an athlete about to compete in the Olympics.

"Okay. As Sharon would say, 'Pitter-patter, let's get at 'er!' " Jules said.

Amanda nodded. She shortened her reins, pushed her legs firmly into Prince Charming's sides, and started down the trail in a wobbly trot.

The trail was wide and easy to see. It wound deeper and deeper into the woods. "Up-down, up-down," Amanda chanted to herself in time with her posting as Prince trotted willingly down the path.

Soon she became aware that the trail had begun to slope uphill. "We must be heading up Thacker Mountain now," she said.

She let Prince trot until he seemed tired. The path had gotten steeper. They ambled along until the trail opened out on a clearing and Amanda found herself at the top of the mountain. There was a metal lookout tower there, where park rangers could watch for forest fires in the dry season. But no cars were around. Amanda was all alone.

"I bet you could see all the way to Memphis from up there," she told Prince Charming. Pleased that she had made it halfway through her leg of the Pony Express, Amanda halted for a moment.

Even at the bottom of the lookout tower, the view was splendid. Amanda could see the whole town of Hickoryville, with the little rectangles of field and pasture all around it. "Prince, look,"

Amanda said excitedly. "I believe I see our house there."

Near the bottom of Thacker Mountain she could see an elbow of the county road that wound its way toward other little towns. At the bend in the road was a small square building, with a long red and white awning extending from it. Amanda recognized it as a Sonic Food Land, a chain of hamburger restaurants. At a Sonic, Amanda knew, you drove your car up and ordered your food by two-way radio.

Suddenly she was incredibly thirsty. Her ride was half over, and all downhill from that point on. Amanda had an idea. "Prince," she said, "I believe I'll just go down to that Sonic over there and get me a Diet Pepsi." She steered Prince Charming toward the trees and headed down the mountain toward the Sonic.

From the top of the mountain, it had looked as if it would be easy to cut through the trees and make a beeline for the restaurant. But halfway down, in the thick of the woods, Amanda wasn't so sure. She had been going steadily downhill for fifteen minutes and still hadn't reached the Sonic.

"I just know it's right near here," she said to reassure herself. But she didn't know it at all. She had judged it a ten-minute walk from the mountaintop. "I guess it was farther away than it looked," Amanda said nervously.

Prince trudged on down the mountainside. Quite

suddenly, the steep slope leveled off, and through the trees, Amanda spotted the Sonic.

Delighted with herself, Amanda patted Prince's neck. "You see, Prince? Sonic Food Land. I told you it was right here." She rode up under the awning, halting in one of the parking bays just as if Prince Charming were a car. Then she leaned over carefully and pushed the button on the intercom. She ordered a Diet Pepsi, then sat waiting for the server to bring it out to her.

A moment later, a girl in a red and white striped uniform carried the soda out on a tray. When she saw a horse parked at the speaker instead of a car, she nearly dropped the tray.

Amanda stifled a giggle. Wait until the other kids heard about this! They would surely be impressed.

"Um . . . th-that'll be a dollar twenty-seven," the girl stammered, staring at Prince Charming.

Amanda handed her two dollars. "Keep the change," she said primly.

Prince Charming turned and gave the girl a curious look. He stuck his nose toward her, snuffling hopefully for a treat. The girl screamed.

"Don't worry," Amanda told her. "He won't hurt you." That was the first time Amanda could remember someone else being more afraid of her horse than she was. It made Amanda feel quite bold.

The girl hurried back into the building. Amanda sipped her drink. When she had finished, she leaned over and set the cup on the tray beside the speaker. For a moment she wondered if she should back out of the parking space like a car or just turn around. But before she could decide, Prince stepped forward, up onto the concrete walkway, and right into the little garden area at its center.

"Oh," Amanda said, startled. Prince had begun to gobble down a decorative plant. Amanda tugged at the reins, but the horse ignored her.

"Hey! You there!" A man wearing a red plastic nametag on his shirt came running from the building, an angry expression on his face. Amanda realized he must be the manager. "You'll have to take that . . . that"—he looked at Prince Charming as if he couldn't quite believe what he was seeing—"*vehicle* out of there right away!" he finished. "Or I'll have to call the police."

Luckily Prince backed up when he saw the man run toward him. Amanda shortened the reins and quickly kicked the horse into a trot, away from the Sonic Food Land. As she headed back into the woods, she began to laugh. "Oh, Prince," she said. "That certainly was an adventure! Just wait until we tell the others."

Amanda rode through the woods in the direction of the trail. She was in high spirits after her Sonic adventure, so it wasn't until she had been riding for a good while that she realized she should have come upon the trail already. Had she passed it without realizing? Amanda pulled Prince to a halt, looking around for some sign that she might be near the trail.

The woods were shrouded in shadow. A cold wind had come up, and the sky had clouded over completely. Shivering, Amanda zipped her jacket all the way up. She started forward again uncertainly, then decided to turn around and retrace her steps.

"I must have crossed the trail and not noticed it," she said to herself. "I'll find it again if I ride back." But when she turned around, there was not one familiar thing in sight.

The cold feeling of dread had returned, bigger than ever. It lay in her stomach, growing ever larger as she walked and walked through the trees and did not recognize anything. "Is anybody out there?" she called. Her voice sounded thin and pitiful in the empty woods. "Can anybody hear me?" she yelled again.

There was no answer. "Just stay on the trail." Jules's words ran through her head, over and over. "Oh, I should have listened," Amanda said fearfully. "I never should have gone off the trail. Now we're lost, Prince."

Amanda began to panic. The trees seemed to be coming alive. They groaned and creaked, swaying in the cold wind. Amanda kicked Prince Charming into a canter. She had no idea where they were headed. She just wanted to get away. She gripped the reins in terror as Prince thundered through the woods.

Suddenly a low tree limb loomed before her. *Steer around it, steer around it,* the little voice inside her said, then *duck!* when it was too late to do anything else.

Prince cantered under the tree limb. The terrified Amanda did not duck. She threw up her arms to protect her face and felt the limb connect with her chest. She grabbed at the limb, wrapping her arms around it, and managed to hold on as the saddle went out from under her. She clung to the branch, her legs dangling in the air. For a sickening moment, she thought she was going to throw up. The sturdy limb had knocked the wind out of her, but somehow she hung on. The ground seemed far below her. She found the strength to kick one leg over the branch, and managed to pull herself up to a precarious sitting position. Then she watched helplessly as Prince Charming cantered away, riderless.

"Prince Charming!" Amanda called desperately. "Prince Charming, come back! Don't leave me here!"

But his hoofbeats grew fainter until they faded away. The only sound was the lonely wind stirring the dry leaves, and the ominous creaking of the bare branches. Amanda began to cry. She was all alone in the darkening woods.

# 11

MEGAN PEERED IMPATIENTLY AT THE TRAIL. AMANDA should have met the group by now, even if she hadn't trotted or cantered much along her route. "Where could she be?" Megan asked, for the thousandth time.

"I don't know," Jake said, "but I'm gettin' worried. This weather is startin' to look worse. The radio says it's goin' to snow."

The horse van was parked beside a little bait shop near the lake. Jake paced back and forth, watching the sky apprehensively.

"Do you think we should call this thing off?" Jenny asked.

"No!" Megan, Max, Keith, and Chloe chorused.

"We're almost done," Megan pleaded. "We'll make it, Jake, I know we will! Even if it snows, we're just an hour and a half ride from town here. How much can it snow in an hour and a half?" she said, in the most logical tone she could manage.

"Well, that's so," Jake said. He crossed the flaps of his jacket over his chest and held them with his folded arms as he began to pace back and forth in front of the trailer. Megan watched him. Every so often, he'd glance toward the end of the trail, where Amanda and Prince Charming should be appearing.

Another ten minutes passed. Jake stopped pacing and announced, "That's it. I'm goin' after her. We're callin' this whole thing off."

"Now, wait a second, Jake," Jules said. "Let's give her a few more minutes. Maybe we just underestimated the time on this leg of the ride."

"And you know Amanda's kind of a weak rider," Megan pointed out. "She's probably just taking her time." Inside, though, Megan had begun to feel guilty. What if Amanda had fallen off and gotten hurt somehow? She began to wish they had all listened to Amanda when she told them she didn't want to ride.

Jake hesitated. Megan seized the moment. "I'll find her, Jake," she said, mounting up on her pony.

"Oh, no you don't," Jake started to protest.

But Megan couldn't stand to sit there waiting another second. She was off before anyone could stop her.

Pixie, who had spent most of the day on the

trailer, was raring to go. The dark gray pony charged eagerly up the trail. Megan let her go for a minute, then she realized she'd better slow down or she might miss Amanda. She brought Pixie back to a trot as she searched the trees around her on both sides.

Quite suddenly, she heard a crashing of branches and crunching of leaves, and Prince Charming's familiar white face appeared in the woods to the right of the trail. But Amanda wasn't on his back. Megan looked past him, hoping to see her straggling along behind. But the woods were empty.

"Prince," Megan called. "Come here, big boy." She walked Pixie up to the horse and cautiously reached for the reins, which were still around Prince's neck. At the last second, Pixie snorted impatiently at him and Prince shied away. But Megan made a grab for the reins and managed to hold on to them.

"Whoa, Prince," she said soothingly. Prince stood still and Megan nudged Pixie forward until she was close enough to take the *mochila* from Prince's back. She slipped it under her seat. She had the *mochila;* now she could finish the Pony Express.

But she also had Prince Charming. Megan hesitated. Should she take Prince Charming back to the trailer, and let the others look for Amanda while she went on? No, Jake would never let her complete the ride with Amanda missing. And Megan was determined to finish.

Her watch said three o'clock. There were only a couple of hours of daylight left, at best. Every minute was beginning to count. She shortened her reins and held them in her right hand, glad she had practiced riding one-handed so many times. She held Prince's reins firmly in her left hand, and with a couple of tugs, got him to follow her. Megan knew what she had to do. She headed off in the direction the horse had come from, to search for Amanda.

Megan picked her way through the woods, winding in and out through the trees. From time to time she called, "Amaaan-da," her voice ringing out through the empty woods. She halted Pixie, listening for a reply. But none came.

Something cold and damp brushed against her cheek. Megan looked up and saw lacy flakes of white drifting down from the sky. It had begun to snow.

"Amaaan-da!" Megan pressed on, beginning to feel anxious. She was running out of time. If she didn't find Amanda soon, she'd never make it back to town by six o'clock. "Amaaan-daaa!" she called, listening hopefully.

Suddenly she thought she heard something. She stopped and cocked her ears, straining to hear it again. Then it came to her, faintly but surely . . . the sound of someone crying.

Megan turned toward the sound and let her ears guide her. The crying grew louder and louder. At last she rode around the twisted roots of an old, fallen tree and her search was over. Clinging to a low branch of a stately old pin oak tree, sobbing brokenheartedly, was Amanda.

Megan halted. "Amanda!" she said.

Amanda slowly lifted her head, hugging the branch. "Megan?" she said in disbelief. "Oh, Megan, I'm so glad to see you!"

"What are you doing up in that tree?" Megan asked.

Amanda told her how Prince had cantered under the limb, which was about as big around as a man's leg, and about six feet off the ground. Amanda was perched precariously over it, several feet from the trunk of the tree.

"You're supposed to bend forward to go under tree limbs," Megan lectured her. "Don't you know that?"

"I do now," Amanda said ruefully. "Can you help me get down from here?"

"Why don't you just jump?" Megan suggested. It wasn't really that far to the ground. Megan wouldn't have hesitated to jump down.

"I'm scared to," Amanda whimpered.

Megan studied the situation. Obviously Amanda was a rookie tree climber. "All right," Megan said. "I'll lead Prince Charming underneath you and you can climb down onto his back."

"Okay," Amanda said doubtfully.

Megan led Prince under the branch. It took some

maneuvering to get him into position, but finally she got him to stand in the right spot. "Okay," Megan called. "Come on down."

"Hold him tight," Amanda said fearfully.

"I've got him," Megan said.

For once Prince was obedient. He stood patiently while Amanda awkwardly felt for the saddle with her feet. Her arms were still locked around the tree limb.

"Okay, drop," Megan said. "You're right over the saddle."

"I can't," Amanda whined.

"Amanda, you have to," Megan told her in a stern voice. "Otherwise, I'm going to leave you in this tree all night."

"No, don't leave!" Amanda closed her eyes, loosened her grip on the limb, and plopped onto Prince Charming's back. When he felt her hit the saddle, he bent his head around and gave her a funny look. *Well, that wasn't too graceful,* his expression seemed to say.

Megan handed Amanda her reins and waited until she got her feet into the stirrups before she said, "Okay, let's go. We haven't got much time."

The girls started off through the woods. After a few minutes, Amanda asked, "Are you sure we're goin' the right direction?"

"Of course I'm sure," Megan said confidently. They trotted on.

The woods grew gloomier as the daylight faded

and the snow began to fall in earnest. Megan thought she had been heading back toward the bait shop, but suddenly she wasn't so sure. She halted, looking around carefully, hoping to spot a familiar tree or her pony's footprints that she could follow back to the trail. But all she saw were mute, gray tree trunks, all alike, and an endless carpet of brown leaves lightly dusted with snow.

"Amanda?" Megan said. "Do you recognize anything around here?"

Amanda's blue eyes were wide with fear. She shook her head.

"I . . . I think we're lost," Megan admitted.

"Oh, no," Amanda wailed. "I thought you said you knew the way!"

"I thought I did," Megan said. "But I must've gotten turned around somehow."

"What'll we do?" Amanda asked fearfully.

"Keep moving," Megan said, trying to sound brave. "Sooner or later we'll find the lake, or the county road. Then we can figure out how to get back into Hickoryville."

They rode on, the woods growing colder and darker as night fell. The snow cast a faint white glow underfoot, but after a while Megan could barely make out the outlines of the trees. More than once, low branches scratched the girls' faces or bumped their helmets. At last they had to dismount and lead the horses. Amanda began to sob helplessly.

Megan felt like crying herself. Once again, she had tried to do the right thing and ended up getting herself into deep trouble. *I shouldn't have ridden off by myself,* she thought miserably. *I should have let Jake find Amanda. Maybe then we could have finished the ride.* She felt like she had let everyone down, especially Allie. Megan shivered, and pulled at the zipper of her jacket, but it was already up as far as it would go. If she hadn't been so rash, she'd already be home in her own warm house. Instead, she was lost in the woods at night in the snow. *Jake must have the police searching for us by now,* Megan figured. But what if the police couldn't find them? What if she and Amanda couldn't find their own way, either? What if they froze to death out there in the cold woods?

Suddenly, Megan saw something that chilled her more than the snowy air. The green eyes of an animal glowed in the dim light.

"What's that?" Amanda asked.

"I don't know." Megan swallowed.

The eyes moved closer. Megan reached for Amanda's arm, and the two girls clutched each other and waited for whatever horrible thing was about to happen to them. What kind of animal was it? Something with sharp fangs? Something that would defend its territory? Something that would attack two girls lost in the scary woods at night?

"Meow?" the animal said. The two eyes blinked

in the darkness. "Meow," it said again. Its voice was loud and peculiar.

Megan began to laugh. "It's just a cat," she said, relief flooding through her. "I guess it's lost, too. Here, kitty," she called.

The cat scampered toward her. It rubbed against her legs. Megan picked it up, feeling its cold feet. The cat purred, pushing its face against Megan's affectionately. Megan could barely see it in the dim light, but there was something funny about it. Then she realized: the cat had no whiskers.

"Poor kitty," Megan said. "Are you lost, too?" She scratched the cat's chin, glad to be holding on to something warm.

Suddenly, it leaped out of her arms.

"Hey!" Megan said, startled. "What's the matter?"

The cat trotted away. Then it turned around, and when it looked back at her, Megan saw its green eyes glowing in the snowlight. "Meow!" it called, its voice loud and insistent.

"Let's follow it," Amanda suggested. "Maybe it's not lost."

"You might be right," Megan said, feeling a tiny bit hopeful.

They tramped through the woods after the cat, leading Pixie and Prince Charming. The cat kept up the same strange behavior, trotting up ahead of Megan and Amanda, then calling out to them in its plaintive mew.

After about ten minutes, Megan became aware

**127**

that it was growing lighter. The trees seemed to be thinning, and she could see more of the gray sky overhead. All of a sudden she glimpsed the warm twinkle of lamplight coming from the window of a house.

"Amanda!" she said excitedly. "Look!"

They had come out of the woods and into an open field. Just beyond the field, Megan saw a row of houses. "We found the town!" Megan said excitedly. The little cat had led them back to Hickoryville.

Megan couldn't see her watch in the darkness, but suddenly she was filled with hope. "Amanda, mount up," she ordered. "Maybe there's still time!"

She gave Amanda a leg up. Then she scooped up the little cat and mounted up on Pixie. With the cat nestled into the crook of her arm, Megan called out, "Come on, Amanda. Let's go!"

They trotted briskly through the snowy field. In minutes, they had ridden through someone's backyard and onto the street. Megan read the signpost at the corner of the street. "Barr Street!" she said. "We're almost there." A minute later they were turning onto Lamar. Megan saw the white courthouse before her and a small crowd of people milling around. The girls trotted on, the horses' feet making no sound on the snow-covered street.

They were two blocks from their destination when the courthouse clock began to chime. "Donggg," it rang out. Megan glanced at the clock face. It was just seconds before six o'clock. "We can still make it!" she said. The clock chimed again. She held the cat firmly in her left arm. "Come on, Amanda, ride!" Megan said. She pushed the reins forward and clucked at Pixie, who began to gallop up the deserted street toward the town square.

"Donggg," the chime rang out. "Donggg," it said again, as Megan and Amanda flew past Phil's Auto Parts, past the cleaners and Hickoryville Savings and Loan. If they could make it to the square before the clock finished chiming, they would have completed the Pony Express ride, and Mr. Sloane would have to give them the money.

"Donggg," said the clock, as the snowflakes swirled around Megan and her pony's feet pounded softly upon the snow. She pressed Pixie's sides, encouraging her to lengthen her stride, and Pixie flew. The pony's legs were a dark blur against the white snow as they passed the office building on the corner and headed toward the crowd in front of the courthouse.

"Look!" someone said.

"Here they come!" said another.

Then Megan heard the whole crowd begin to cheer her on as she galloped to the center of the square. Pixie's feet scattered a spray of snow over the crowd as she came to a halt, just as the six o'clock chime rang out from the courthouse clock.

"We made it, we made it!" Megan crowed. She

looked for Amanda and leaned over to give her a high five.

"Megan!" someone called. She spotted Chloe, Max, and Keith in the crowd.

"We're so glad you're okay!" Chloe said. "When you didn't come back to the bait shop, Jake sent us here with Jules and the trailer in case you finished the route. He called the police, and they're out searching for you," Chloe said soberly.

"We'd better find a phone and let them know we're okay," Megan said.

Then Mr. Sloane appeared. He had been waiting in his car. He didn't seem happy at all. Instead, he just looked annoyed that he had to come out in the snow. He tromped up the steps of the platform and, forcing a smile onto his scowling face, announced that the Pony Express ride was complete. "And now," he said, "I will read the important message that these brave riders have carried. Just as the Pony Express brought the news of the election of Abraham Lincoln across the continent over a hundred years ago, our Pony Express has carried this valuable statement."

Mr. Sloane took the blue envelope from the *mochila* and opened it up. Everyone waited to hear what the message was. Mr. Sloane cleared his throat. "Vote for Gerald R. Sloane for mayor!" he read triumphantly.

The people clapped politely. Then Mr. Sloane presented the Short Stirrup Club with a check for five thousand dollars. "Here's your donation," he said grumpily.

"Thanks, Daddy," Amanda said.

"Thanks, Mr. Sloane," the other kids chimed.

"Thanks, kitty," Megan whispered to the little cat with no whiskers that she still held in her left arm.

Mr. Sloane dismissed them with a wave and got into his car. "Hurry up and put that horse away, Amanda," he said. "It's cold out here, dad-gummit!"

By the time the search for Megan and Amanda had been called off, and the horses blanketed, fed, and put away for the night, Megan was more tired than she could believe. But she was also more proud of herself than she had ever been in her life. "This is even better than winning a championship in a horse show," Megan told her parents that night.

The next day the Short Stirrup Club visited Allie in the hospital. They told her about their Pony Express ride and presented her with the money they'd raised: ten thousand dollars.

"So you can go back to farrier school when you're well," Megan told her.

"Y'all did that for me?" Allie whispered. She looked at them in disbelief.

Sharon had come with them. "Jake and I talked it over, Allie," Sharon told her, "and we want you to come stay with us until your hands get better. We've got plenty of room in that old house."

"I can't believe it," Allie said. "You're the best friends I've ever had."

"Allie, Thistle Ridge Farm just wouldn't be the same without you," Sharon said sincerely.

"There's one more friend here who wants to say hello," Megan said mysteriously. She nodded at Chloe, who was hiding something under her coat.

Chloe came forward, the coat wiggling. "Meow?" came a small cry from under the coat. A tabby-striped head popped up. It was a little cat, whose whiskers seemed to have been singed off in a fire.

"Bandit!" Allie cried joyously. The cat leaped out of the coat and settled on top of Allie's chest, purring mightily.

Allie's eyes blurred with tears as she cuddled the cat who had saved her life awkwardly in her arms. She couldn't speak, but she looked up at each child, and her eyes told them how grateful she was.

At last Allie said, "You know, when my house burned down, I thought I lost everything that was important. But all that really matters is right here in this room. And I thank you all for showing me that."

"You guys really did it this time," Sharon said warmly.

Megan grinned at Max, who elbowed Keith, who scuffed his foot at Chloe, who nudged Amanda, who for once took the initiative. She put out her hand, and one by one, the others piled their hands on top.

"Short Stirrup Club!" they cheered. And Sharon and Allie cheered with them.

# About the Author

ALLISON ESTES grew up in Oxford, Mississippi. She wrote, bound, and illustrated her first book when she was five years old, learned to drive her grandfather's truck when she was eight, and got her first pony when she was ten. She has been writing, driving trucks, and riding horses ever since.

Allison is a trainer at Claremont Riding Academy, the only riding stable in New York City. She currently lives in Manhattan with her eight-year-old daughter, Megan, who spends every spare moment around, under, or on horses.

# STORIES FOR EVERY HORSE LOVER

## By Anne Eliot Crompton

### The Snow Pony

Janet is new in town, and has no friends. Then she gets a job caring for a wild pony. But when it's time for the pony to be given away, will Janet be alone again? Or has she learned how to make friends and keep them?

### The Rainbow Pony

Alice and Jinny are best friends, but Jinny is very bossy, and Alice doesn't like to fight. Then one day Alice rescues a pony, but her father has a "no animals" rule so she secretly keeps it at Jinny's place. Soon Alice will have to take care of the pony herself—even if it means standing up to her dad and Jinny, too.

### The Wildflower Pony

The sequel to *The Rainbow Pony*

Alice's pony surprises her by giving birth to a foal. How can she ever afford to feed *two* ponies? Then she hears about the Fourth of July contest. The best animal act will be awarded $500. With two adorable ponies and lots of practice, Alice is sure she can win. But if she doesn't, will she still be able to keep the foal?

A MINSTREL® BOOK
Published by Pocket Books